"Abby, there are ta~~rget reasons~~ I can't do an interview."

He held up his hand. "But I can't tell you what they are, so don't ask."

"I promise whatever you say won't leave this room." She watched him for any break in the set of his stubborn features. Nothing. "I want to help you. Just tell me what's holding you back, so we can fix it."

At her heartfelt plea, his expression shifted. She'd never beheld a more tortured visage. Still, he wouldn't meet her gaze.

Abby reached out and squeezed his hand. "Please."

Jeremy pulled back. "Don't you think I want to? I can't."

"Fine. You win. That's the last time I'll beg you to share something with me that you won't."

"Can't."

"We're done here."

He paused beside her in the doorway. "Abby—"

"Goodbye, Pastor Walker." Abby closed the door and leaned against it, biting her fist to keep the tears at bay. She'd never show him how deep his silence cut into her soul. Never.

KD Fleming worked in a number of jobs before realizing she had the heart of a storyteller. She lives in west central Florida with her husband of sixteen years. They enjoy fishing, yard work and cheering on their favorite college team when not looking for snow in the Great Smoky Mountains or relaxing on the balcony of a cruise ship. KD loves reading and working with her three critique partners.

KD FLEMING

Capturing the Minister's Heart

HEARTSONG
PRESENTS

Recycling programs
for this product may
not exist in your area.

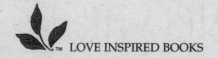 LOVE INSPIRED BOOKS

ISBN-13: 978-0-373-48770-7

Capturing the Minister's Heart

www.Harlequin.com

Printed in U.S.A.

Do nothing out of selfish ambition or vain conceit.
Rather, in humility value others above yourselves.
—*Philippians 2:3*

Thank you to God for His mercy and love.

To my wonderful husband, Frank, for our "guy speak" sessions and your faith in me to write the best book I can. You give me reasons to love you more each day.

To my critique partners—Carol Post, Sabrina Jarema and Dixie Taylor—thank you for your honest and priceless feedback. And for being my dear, dear friends. You'll always be beyond compare in my heart.

To my wonderful agent, Nalini Akolekar, and my fabulous editor, Kathy Davis. Both of you inspire me to reach higher with your belief in my stories. You are both the greatest.

And last, but hardly least, is our very own Abby. Your pure heart and strong faith helped me make the Abby on the page a real and godly woman. I love you, Abby Darlin'.

Chapter 1

Abby Blackmon shot Pastor Jeremy Walker the evil eye as she snatched the finance committee's proposal off the protective glass covering of his desk. She stuffed it into her briefcase. His office usually evoked a sense of comfort. The cherry-stained furnishings complemented the lush gold textured carpet, creating a sense of timeless assurance. *Hopefulness*.

But today, Jeremy's unexplained recalcitrance filled her with an irritation no peaceful ambiance could quell. She regarded the thicker theological tomes lining his bookshelves with an eye toward their physical, rather than spiritual, effectiveness. As in, the best one to use to knock some sense into his stubborn head.

"We need to get the community behind this project if we're going to raise the money to build the recreation center. The indoor center *you* want built. Remember? The outreach ministry for disadvantaged kids? A place their parents could send them during the hot, humid summer and know they were safe. Ring any bells for you?"

He opened his mouth as if to answer her. But nothing came out. He wouldn't even meet her gaze. Instead, he angled his leather chair to her left and looked out the window. A serious air befitting the responsibilities of his calling cloaked him like a heavy trench coat. He was tall, athletic, with an expressive face anchored by a strong jaw, best captured in profile. His sandy-brown hair always looked as if he'd just run his hands through it, which he did now instead of explaining himself. He swiveled his chair and faced her. His eyes, usually more gold than green, and glinting with humor to balance the mien of seriousness, were a flat shade of brown. Their somberness didn't offer her any hope of changing his mind.

Still, she tried. "Jeremy, giving interviews and wooing the media is how my father's campaign manager raises the most funds for his re-election. They share their vision with the people who have a vested interest in reaching the same goal, and then they gain their support."

His mouth opened. "I—" He fell silent again.

"You have to give me a better reason for rejecting a proposal the finance committee spent weeks working on. 'No interviews' isn't good enough, and you know it."

Their glares waged a silent war. Despite her determination, she blinked first. That loosened his rigid posture and he leaned back in his chair, his jaw clamped shut.

"Fine," she said. "You can explain yourself to the committee at the end of the month. But know this—I've dealt with difficult people before. And despite them, the project was finished on time."

The normally agreeable—until today—minister repositioned his rimless glasses. Probably so his view would be focused when he looked down his nose at her. At Grace Community Church, his word was final in the hierarchy of decision making. Never mind that he was being nonsensical with his "no cameras and no interviews" edict. She glanced at her watch. Great. Katherine was probably already at the restaurant, wondering where she was.

Abby stood, straightening a crease in her pencil skirt, stalling until she had her temper under control. "My parents asked me to invite you to dinner at their house this Saturday. Daddy's due back in Washington next week."

Her gaze sought his when he didn't respond. "I won't be there, if that's the reason for your hesitation."

Jeremy ran a hand through his hair again and let out a soul-deep sigh. "Please, tell your parents I'm happy to have dinner with them." He watched her for a moment before clearing his throat. "I know you and the committee worked hard on this proposal, but I won't change my mind about the interviews. I *am* sorry, Abby. You'll have to find another way."

She nodded. "I'll let them know to expect you." At the door, she placed her hand on the knob before glancing back at him. "And I don't believe you are. Sorry, that is." She walked out, leaving the door gaping open like the invisible chasm separating them.

Disappointment dogged her on the drive to the restaurant. She'd stopped by Jeremy's office with the idea of giving him a brief rundown of the proposal, then leaving it with him for further review. He would, of course, love it, then call her later in the week about scheduling the interviews. So much for great ideas or thinking they were on the same page about anything.

A few minutes later, Abby slid into the booth across from her friend Katherine Harper. She snapped her linen napkin open with a loud pop, wincing when Katherine glanced up from her menu. "Sorry."

Del Sol boasted cozy privacy, where the booths scattered around the expansive room invited long and lingering conversations. They were using an extended lunch hour to put the final touches on the plans for Katherine's upcoming wedding, in which Abby was her maid of honor and Jeremy was officiating. That one thought reignited her anger.

As soon as the waiter had taken their orders, Katherine leaned forward. "What's wrong?"

Abby's gaze flew to hers. "Nothing."

Katherine reached over and rescued the saucer of butter pats from the salad fork Abby was wielding like a pitchfork. Each golden decorative floral design had been transformed into a thin, round blob riddled with enough holes that it could pass for Swiss cheese.

"What's the matter?" Katherine used her patient, logical voice on her.

Oh, how Abby hated the sound of obvious reason. Katherine wouldn't talk about anything else, even her perfect wedding to Mr. Dreamy, if she didn't pour all this vexation out and let Katherine try to fix it. Which she couldn't. No one could but the stubborn minister whose jaw had turned to granite right after the word *no* had passed his lips.

"Fine." Once she began tattling on Jeremy, the words wouldn't stop. Then, finally she said, "He refused to participate in any interviews involving cameras. No television, no newspaper reports."

"Our Jeremy?"

"He might be yours. But he is definitely not mine. Not after this morning." She snagged a piece of bread before Katherine could move that out of reach, too.

"That is so odd." Katherine scrunched her brow and took a sip from her water glass. "He has always been a clown. But now that you mention it, I don't think I've ever seen him pose for a picture. In fact, he finds an excuse to leave the room just before we take group photos with the church outreach volunteers."

"You should have seen him. He acted so angry with me. It was as if I'd asked him to keep the car running while I robbed the bank instead of being interviewed for a local news feature." Abby sank farther into her seat. "I don't know where I'm supposed to go from here. That was *the* plan."

Katherine slid the butter dish toward her. An act of pity Abby wouldn't acknowledge.

"And the way he looked down his nose at me. Oh, I wanted to just shake him until he saw how ridiculous he was being." The fresh-baked bread on her plate hadn't fared any better than the pats of butter. "You don't think it's a phobia, do you?"

"More like camera shyness. I mean, he has no trouble with public speaking. I don't see where having his picture in the paper would be nearly as scary as standing in front of five hundred church members each Sunday and reminding them that God sees everything they do or say."

Abby leaned forward. "I checked Google on my phone before I came inside. But all I found were articles relating to archaic religious or spiritual superstitions."

"What? How can a minister have a spiritual issue with a camera?"

She laughed, and some of her frustration faded. "The person believes that when the camera captures their image, it's also capturing their soul."

They both leaned back as the waiter placed their salads in front of them.

After saying grace, Katherine stabbed a forkful of grilled chicken and greens. "My vote's still on camerashyness."

"Are you using me to practice up on how to inject political jargon into conversations like any good politician's wife-to-be?"

Katherine stuck her tongue out at her, and the topic of conversation switched from Jeremy to all things wedding. Abby noted the appointment time in her planner for their final dress fittings. Nick was picking up the invitations as soon as the printer said they were done.

"Oh, we need a sample of the fabric from your

dresses to give to the florist so he can match it to the ribbons in the bouquets. Please don't let me forget that when we're there."

Abby glanced up, her pen poised over the planner page, and smiled. "Look at you. Ready to write an article for a bridal magazine on the importance of matching colors."

"Pfft. That isn't what I'm doing and you know it. If you and Gina don't go with me, the florist will have talked me into having you both walk down the aisle carrying a crystal vase full of roses that resemble a rainbow."

The sad thing was it was the truth. Kat had confessed to her that Nick had promised this florist exclusive rights to their wedding in exchange for coordinating the floral part of his wooing campaign to win her heart.

Thoughts of how happy the two of them were going to be soon had Abby cramming Jeremy and his prickliness into the "to be dealt with later" part of her brain. She immersed herself in helping her best friend plan the wedding of her dreams to her Prince Charming.

After they'd gone through both their lists, coordinating times and things still needing attention, the waiter cleared their dishes from the table. Katherine insisted on picking up the check in thanks for Abby helping keep her on target. Abby hugged her goodbye in the parking lot before heading to her office.

Once there, she pulled the wrinkled pages of her plan to make Jeremy's dream come true from her briefcase and threw them in the trash. All she'd lost with her impromptu meeting this morning was an easy way to raise money for the rec center—and any hope she had that Jeremy saw her as something more than a member of the finance committee and the church he pastored. It was better she knew his position on both, now, before she invested any more effort into a doomed venture.

She had always admired him and the heavy burden he carried in his heart, not just for his congregation, but all of Pemberly, Georgia. With the numerous programs they had worked on together, she'd thought she knew him. But the man who'd shot down her ideas before she could get out of the starting gate today wasn't her Jeremy, willing to do whatever it took to meet the needs of his people. This morning's Jeremy had been a cold and distant stranger.

Her Jeremy—oh, goodness, she had not just thought of him that way. They were friends. They respected each other's views. And, yes, she had hoped that sometime in the near future their relationship would grow into something deeper. At least she had until today's face-off.

Oh, she was pathetic. What kind of person had warm, fuzzy flutters in her heart when she thought about her pastor? She was sick. Sick, sick, sick. *God, help me. You're the only one who can.*

To distract her from her crazy thoughts and find a way around Jeremy's edicts, she scrolled through her contacts list, on the hunt for someone to help raise the money to begin construction. Because, no matter how many ideas Jeremy rejected, she was the head of the finance committee tasked with gaining the necessary funding to see this project completed. She always achieved her goals. And she would this time, too—with or without Pastor Jeremy Walker's nod of approval and help.

Halfway down the screen she spotted Wendy Albright's name. *Oh, yes.* Wednesday Wendy hosted midweek features involving the community for Channel Six News. Perfect. Abby's father hadn't recommended she attend the University of Georgia just because it was his alma mater. She'd met and forged friendships with people who were now influential members of society throughout the state and the country. Including Wendy.

Ten minutes later, she was explaining her "need" to her fellow sorority Faithful Sister.

"Abby, darlin', if we Faithfuls can't help each other out, what is this world coming to?"

She smiled. Wendy was just as Southern as ever. Some things never changed. "Exactly. I'm trying to raise money for a church-based recreation center that would also benefit the community. Do you know of any eager philanthropists willing to have their name on a bronze plaque over the top of the double doors when we dedicate the building to the city of Pemberly?"

"What's your angle in wanting it built?"

Abby sat up straight. "The community needs this for the teens. The church has an outdoor court for basketball, but with all the rain and heat during summer, it's hard to get the kids out of the AC long enough to make a difference in their lives."

"Hmm. Basketball, you said? I know a former Hawks player with a soft heart for community projects that benefit kids. He's only been out of the game a few years, so his name would still be a big draw. Give me your number, and I'll ask him to call you. You aren't married, are you?"

"What? Why does that matter?"

"He's a bit of a lady's man, but he's harmless. If I don't use *Mrs.* anywhere in your name, he'll call you back faster. I've interviewed him a few times. He's really a nice guy. But he likes the time spent with the people asking him for a donation to include something besides bringing his checkbook and them offering him a pen. Be charming and talk about more than the project when you take him out to dinner."

Abby laughed and gave Wendy her contact information. "I think I remember how to play the Southern belle. Give him my number with the promise of a great dinner and a concert thrown in for good measure if he calls me back this week."

"Will do. But seriously, Abby Blackmon, attorney-at-law and daughter of a senator, really doesn't have anyone special?"

The image of solemn hazel eyes and tousled hair flashed in her mind, and she forced the words past the squeezing pressure around her heart. "No, there's no one special for me."

"That's just wrong." Then, after an abbreviated silence, "I hate to run, but I'm due on set for a sound check in five. Call me after construction begins. I'll see what kind of feature coverage I can arrange for your pet project and the basketball star. Who knows, maybe you'll get more than a rec center out of the introduction."

"I really appreciate your help, but a sponsor for the rec center is all I'm after right now." After hanging up, she twisted her chair around until she could see the fountain in the middle of the park across the street. She let out a relieved sigh and smiled with satisfaction. If things worked out, she might have found the perfect "face" to promote the rec center project and an interesting dinner companion. Not that she was looking.

Late Friday afternoon, Jeremy came into the fellowship hall to help set up for the weekly meal for the homeless. He'd switched schedules with three different members of the congregation during the rest of the week to avoid running into Abby. No one was willing to trade their Friday night out for kitchen duty, though. There was no escaping her or their shift on dish washing detail after the meal.

The kitchen in the fellowship hall was roomy. But the sinks were side by side. Earlier, while she'd worked the serving line, Abby had said "thank you" with a sweet smile and warmth in her silver-blue eyes each time he'd brought her a refill for the mashed potatoes or green beans. She hadn't shown a single sign of irritation over his harsh rejection of her plans. But now all the food was gone, and so was the buffer the other volunteers provided. It was just the two of them and a pile of dirty dishes.

No one liked kitchen cleanup. Except Abby. She viewed the task as part of the job instead of torture. She had a soft spot for the less fortunate in their town. She delighted in meeting and making welcome any new-comers to the dinner crowd. The regulars looked for her and her warm smile as they made their way down the serving line, and she never disappointed. The care and attention she showed each person drew their spine a little straighter and raised their opinion of the meal from charity to dinner with a friend.

Jeremy didn't know if he was in that category any longer. She had been furious when she'd left his of-fice Monday. And they hadn't seen or spoken to each other since. Both situations were his fault. That truth wouldn't make the next hour any less uncomfortable.

He ran the hot water, creating high peaks of frothy suds before dumping all the silverware into the left sink. Abby had yet to speak to him on a personal level. No asking how his week had been or commenting on the size of tonight's crowd. If he wanted to dispel the silence hovering between them, he'd have to start the conversation. He grabbed a moment and really looked at her, taking in her golden, sun-kissed complexion, heart-shaped face made more beautiful by the glint of mischief in her expressive eyes and those full lips. Her physical beauty was only a reflection of her spiri-tual loveliness.

He swallowed hard. "I think there were more new-comers tonight than we've had in a while."

She was humming one of the choir standards as she wiped the stainless counter where the serving pans had rested earlier. She paused at his words, glancing in his direction. "There were thirteen new faces."

Okay, he deserved to have to work at making their exchange into an actual conversation. "Abby, I'm sorry I upset you at the meeting. It's just—"

She waved him off. "Don't worry about it. I can't say I understand your reasons for not doing all you can to reach the youth in our city. But that's for you to deal with. I've found an even better way to raise the money. And the church should qualify for a loan for the amount necessary to finish construction if we use the property as collateral."

What? They were talking about a huge amount of money. "It only took you four days to come up with a better way to raise hundreds of thousands of dollars?"

"Uh-huh. Can you pass me that towel so I can dry these spoons?"

He handed her the towel but held on when she pulled. "What have you done? I know my refusal upset you. But I'm not doing any interviews. Not even for you."

The gentle squeeze she gave his shoulder was the equivalent of a pat on the head for a dog that had mastered the trick of rolling over on command. He gritted his teeth. "How are you raising the money, Abby?"

"Why all this sudden interest in my methods? You were quick to let me know the easiest avenue to achieving this goal was off-limits. So I did as you asked and took you out of the equation."

"I don't want to fight with you about this."

"We're not fighting. I was just letting you know I took your advice and found another way to move ahead." She turned away and started humming again.

He stared at the back of her head, the tether of their friendship loosening in the silence. He sighed. He deserved her dismissal. But he didn't have to like it. Rules that had held him captive for more than a decade prevented him from doing what she needed on a project he knew in his heart was what God wanted for their city. He should be glad she was able to work around the obstacles he'd thrown in her way.

She didn't act vindictive or even satisfied, as if she was getting back at him for shutting down her original plan. She looked—happy, without him in the picture. He steeled himself against reacting to the sharp jolt that lanced through him at her assurance that everything was progressing just fine without him.

They had always gotten along, making a great team when addressing the financial needs of the church. Abby was creative and expansive when it came to problem-solving or fund-raising. But he couldn't allow his face to appear in any form of media, no matter how logical and well thought out her proposal had been. And he couldn't explain why. It was against the Witness Security Program's and Marshal Dekker's rules.

"Are you going to make me wait until the next finance committee meeting?"

She spread the drying towel she had been using across the handle of the oven, then reached for a new one before facing him. "I spoke to a college friend who put me in touch with Shaun Fowler. He's big into community projects for kids. Especially anything to do with basketball. Anyway, I met him for dinner last night, and we talked—"

"Wait right there." He threw his scouring pad into the sink, sending a plume of suds high into the air. "Shaun Fowler, the former Atlanta Hawks player? You went out with him?"

He should have interpreted the lift of her perfectly shaped eyebrow and the firm set of her full lips as a warning. Even without her arms folded tightly in front of her. It didn't matter. His vision was passing through a haze of green. He stepped closer until there was less than an arm's length between them. "Fundraising should not include your having to schmooze people into donating for a cause. Especially playboy pro athletes."

She looked up at him, the top of her head almost level with his chin and her back ramrod straight. "Schmooze a playboy? I had dinner with a handsome man who happens to like giving money to worthy causes. Since I chair the committee tasked with raising the funds to build the recreation center *you*—" she poked him in the chest with a fingernail as sharp as her words "—asked us to take on, I am doing my job. And I won't apologize for having a pleasant evening in the company of a man who doesn't have any odd hang-ups."

She stalked away to fill the slotted drawer with the dried silverware. Jeremy's chest was heaving like a stovepipe. He wanted nothing more than to make her face him and explain exactly how pleasant her evening had been. But he had no right. No claim. Dekker and the rules made sure of that. Never mind how angry he'd made her at their meeting. But the minute he severed the link holding Abby anywhere near him, some former NBA superstar was there, ready to offer her everything he never could because that hadn't been God's plan for his life.

And that hurt.

The realization tore a jagged path from his heart to his soul. He would never be completely separated from her because of their shared friendships with Katherine Harper and Nick Delaney. Suddenly the aridness of a WITSEC relocation spot in Tempe sounded appealing.

God knew what was best for him and for Abby. He had just never let himself consider the possibility that what was best for them wouldn't involve the same path. But maybe it didn't. *Lord, I'm sorry for my selfishness. Please, forgive me and help me to mend this rift I've created between Abby and me. She's my friend, and if Your will doesn't allow for more than that, help me to accept it and cherish the relationship You have blessed us with as friends.*

He swallowed hard. "I'm sorry. I shouldn't have acted that way."

She paused with a long-tined fork in her hand. "No, you shouldn't have. What I do is my business. I'm respecting your edict that I keep the media away from you, but I need a face to associate with this project for people to identify with it. Shaun brings notoriety and good press, not to mention over half the money we need. He's funded similar projects like this all over the country. And he's a nice man. He and I have to work together on promoting the center, so it makes it easier for me that he's so likable."

Abby's gaze shifted before meeting his. "He wants

to stop by and watch you work with the teens one Tuesday evening."

Over his dead body. The guy was not only luring Abby away from him with his charitable works and likability, now the man wanted to get in the middle of the ministry that let him use the skills he had been forced to keep hidden from the world. Great. The guy would probably challenge him to a game of one-on-one in front of the teens. He clenched his fists at his sides. If he got smeared, what credibility would his teaching have in the future?

"Since when did one dinner garner such attention from a former NBA All-Star? Are you sure Shaun Fowler isn't just looking to add a senator's daughter to his collection of adoring female fans?"

His barb brought Abby front and center. She was in his face with her cheeks flushed, strands of honey-gold hair escaping its clip, ready to give him the set down of his life. And she'd never looked more beautiful.

"Get. Over. Yourself. You can't have it both ways. Whatever your fear is that keeps you from doing what's needed to get this center built is your problem. I found a way to move forward despite you. And since your favorite sport is basketball, I went with that theme. And who better to promote our cause than a former NBA player who favors charities that sponsor projects like this? He'll help me draw in the sponsorship we need to make *your* dream happen."

He stepped away from her and leaned against the sink. "I'm sorry."

She shook her head and rolled her eyes. How many

times had he said those words to her this week, knowing he couldn't change anything even if he wanted to?

"There are things I wish I knew how to explain, but I don't. Can't. And I know my attitude resembles sour grapes." The rules might keep him from talking about witness protection, but nothing prevented him from letting her see the path he'd planned for himself before Dekker's late-night visit took all of that away.

He drew a deep breath and bared as much of his soul as he could, with no motive other than hoping she'd understand his mixed feelings a little better. "When I was in high school, all I dreamed about was playing for Kentucky and winning a national championship. I was going to be a first-round draft pick in the NBA." He resisted the resentment trying to climb inside him again at the thought of all he had lost. He'd surrendered that battle to God before attending seminary and won. So why the resentful rumblings now?

Abby's gaze was warm and encouraging.

"But that wasn't what God wanted me to do. And I'm fine with that now. I like being a minister. I think I make a difference in people's lives, helping open their hearts and minds to what God really wants for them."

"You do." Her words a breathy assurance, while her gaze strayed from his. "God used you to open *my* eyes to how much more I should be doing to help others. I'll always be grateful to you for that."

His breath seized in his chest. Was there an underlying meaning in her words? Was she telling him he was just her minister? What about their friendship? He had no choice but to trust God here. He was so far out in a sea of emotion he couldn't see land.

"You have a very giving heart. I think God was already at work within you before our paths crossed. Basketball is how I get the older boys' attention. They think they know everything, and the only way to break through that 'king of the world' mind-set is to outdo them at something. With basketball, when I win, they can always say it's because I've been playing longer or something like that, but it still earns me a little of their respect. And that allows me to plant a seed. God waters it and lets it work deeper into their souls through life's twists and turns, until one day, it finds root and they stand tall, grounded in Him."

Abby stared at Jeremy, listening to the words tumbling from his mouth. He was always so earnest, so passionate in his sermons. There was no doubt about his belief in what he was saying. But just now, with his breath coming in uneven measures, he had opened up and shared a piece of his heart with her that she believed few people had ever seen. The honesty made her want to take him in her arms and tell him how good and honorable he was.

But the type of relationship they had didn't give her the freedom to express that level of admiration. And it might never. Oh, they'd still attend many of the same public functions. They might even go to some of them together if they were low-key enough. Her parents would always invite him to lunch with them on the Sundays they were in town. But she and Jeremy had never been close enough to trade secrets that involved their hearts. Now she wasn't sure they ever could.

They were casual friends. Somehow, he always made her laugh. But they'd never talked about their dreams or a future, whether separate or together. She already missed the friend who couldn't be more.

She offered her hand. "Truce?"

He reached out. But instead of a handshake, he wove his fingers through hers and kissed her knuckles before letting go. "Truce."

Her heart jumped. Frustrating and confusing man!

She went home more flustered than she'd been before the evening started. He kept her off kilter. Probably not on purpose, but that didn't matter. His actions contradicted themselves. One minute he talked to her as if she was the ideal woman—his Eve. The next, he was cranky and suspicious, acting as if he'd caught her two-timing him. She'd never even one-timed him.

She shook off her conflicting thoughts. There'd be time to worry later about the jiggly feeling stirred by the thought of Jeremy jealous over her. Convinced she could find the solution on her own, she struggled with her uncertainty for another hour before giving in and doing what she should have done before any of this happened.

She prayed.

She prayed while she showered. While starting a second load of laundry as the towels dried in the dryer. Even while she painted her toenails Romantic Red. Then she curled up with a cup of tea and poured her heart out to the only one who knew the cause of the hurt and confusion welling up inside her. Who could offer her a solution. Who could bring her peace. Perfect peace. She went to bed after surrendering her plans to God. And she slept. Because the Lord carried her burdens for her through the night as He promised He always would.

Chapter 2

When Abby awoke the next morning, she had a plan. She called Shaun and invited him to come with her to an amateur league game the next weekend instead of meeting the teens on Tuesday. Maybe if he and Jeremy met in a nonthreatening environment, Jeremy would be more receptive to the help Shaun was offering. She noted the schedule change in her calendar before hurrying to pick up Kat and Gina for their fittings with the dressmaker.

Katherine was a vision of happiness in her bridal finery, standing mannequin still while her hem was being pinned.

"As maid of honor, I'm responsible for throwing you a personal shower."

Kat tried twisting her upper body toward her while encased in a gazillion yards of white tulle and almost fell off the small pedestal. Madame Merisel circled her, with her supply of straight pins caught between her lips. Kat's wobble earned her a garbled scolding in French. Abby didn't offer a translation. Some things Kat didn't need to know.

"How personal?" The expression on Kat's face was wary at best.

Just then, Gina, Kat's assistant and their mutual friend, came out in her light turquoise bridesmaid dress and twirled around for them. "It's going to be way more personal than you'd like."

Kat shot Gina a squinted glare, but Gina waved her off. "It's fine. It will be just us women, and we buy you pretty little girlie things to wear on your honeymoon."

When Kat was still frowning, Gina huffed. "Or, we can all give you gift cards and let you go buy out Victoria's Secret alone. Not that you would know how to get there without me drawing you a map. Shopping isn't exactly one of your hobbies."

"Just quit already. It's fine for you guys to give me a shower if you really want to do that. But to be honest, you two are my true friends. I don't want to sit in a circle opening really personal presents from people who don't even know what size I wear. And I am *not* sharing that kind of information with anyone. Can't we just take a day, go to the spa, have a lavish lunch and then go shopping together?"

Abby giggled. There was no helping it, with the nervous look on Kat's face. But what she suggested was perfect. "I think that's a great idea. And since it's my job to make sure the bride's happy and gets whatever she wants for her day, I'll book us a Saturday at the spa two weeks before the wedding. Do you want lunch at Del Sol or Cristo's?"

"Oh, pick Cristo's, please. I love those mini croissants drizzled with icing that they bring while you're waiting for your entree." Gina was nearly bouncing in her strappy sandals.

Kat grinned. "I have this overwhelming craving for Cristo's. It just hit me."

They all laughed until they were almost in tears. Madame Merisel helped Kat step down off the pedestal.

Abby cupped Katherine's face before giving her a big hug. "I am so happy for you. You and Nick are going to be perfect together." Somehow, thoughts of Jeremy invaded this special moment, robbing her of the joy of sharing in her friend's dream come true. She burst into tears.

Madame Merisel had Katherine out of her dress and into a robe before Abby's mascara had time to drip from an eyelash and threaten the silky white creation. Gina stuffed a tissue into Abby's hand, and then she and Kat both rubbed soothing circles along her shoulders until she was done crying.

"I'm so sorry. I don't know what came over me." Abby sniffed and wiped her eyes one last time before shaking off the sudden bout of sadness that had consumed her.

"Is everything okay with you and Jeremy?" Kat drew her close.

Abby's gaze locked with hers. "How—"

"Seriously, there's another man on the planet with the power to make you cry?"

No more was said until Gina was back from changing out of her gown, and Abby was up on the raised platform, her hem being pinned. "I found a new way to raise the money for the recreation center, and Jeremy doesn't like it either."

"Jeremy is the one who said no to being interviewed. Does this involve him being near a camera?" Kat asked in her matter-of-fact, logical way.

"No, it involves me spending time with Shaun Fowler, a former Atlanta Hawks player."

Gina almost spit her bottled water across the room and dabbed at the dribble on her chin. "Oh, my goodness. He *is* gorgeous. My nephew is still crazy about him and has one of those life-size posters of him on the wall in his room. That man looks as good dressed up for dinner as he does sweaty and dripping after a hard game."

Katherine raised her eyebrow in silent question at Abby.

"He is nice, and his organization does a lot to give kids from lower-income families a chance to play sports, especially basketball. I've invited him to come with me to watch the guys play next Saturday."

"Oh, boy."

"Gina, it isn't a big deal." Abby's gaze met hers in the mirror.

"And this is the part of the idea Jeremy isn't okay with," Katherine said.

"I don't know. I didn't tell him Shaun is coming to the game."

With the seamstress's help, Abby wiggled out of the form-fitting gown without a single poke from a stray pin. She let out a relieved breath as she tucked her blouse into her slacks. Katherine and Gina were waiting by the door when she came out of the changing room.

"You have to tell him." Katherine nailed her while she was still ten feet away.

"Why? Shaun will be my guest, and we'll be sitting with you."

As they stepped outside the shop, Gina said, "And me."

"You never come to the games," Abby pointed out as she unlocked the car.

Gina shrugged and got in the front seat. "All the good-looking guys were taken—until now."

Abby's eyes widened. "You would be interested in Shaun?"

"Hello, earth to Abby. He's gorgeous. He's rich. He's nice to small children. Have him bring a puppy, and I'll propose right there."

Katherine whacked her from the backseat. "I can't believe you just said that."

Gina turned around to answer Katherine while Abby started the car. "Isn't that how Nick got you? But I guess if Shaun's Abby's guest, he's taken already."

Abby was through discussing her invitation to Shaun and stayed silent as they headed to their next stop. She glanced in the rearview mirror and caught Katherine's frown.

"What?"

Kat raised her hands, palms outward. "I'm not trying to tell you what you should or shouldn't do, but if Jeremy was upset when you mentioned dinner with Shaun, don't you think you should at least warn him the guy's coming to watch his team play?"

"No, I don't. Because no matter what I do, Jeremy is going to find fault with it. If I don't tell him and just do it, then at least I will have accomplished something before I receive my weekly lecture." Abby signaled and moved into the turn lane. "I'm attracted to Jeremy." She pinned Gina with a "not a word" glare. "I have been. He's one of the finest men I know, on top of being handsome. I'm not afraid to admit that to y'all, but the way he reacted to the whole camera thing really upset me. It was as if I were talking to a stranger. And now things are awkward between us."

Gina was twitching with the effort to suppress her innate nosiness. "Awkward how?"

"Last week he traded shifts with three different people just to avoid me. Then last night he had no choice. It was our turn to do cleanup, so he was stuck in the kitchen with nowhere to run. He apologized for the tension between us and then shared some really deep things from his past. But the whole time he talked, it was like he was listing the reasons why I shouldn't be around him." She let out an anguished sigh. "I'm not sure he wants me as a friend anymore. I prayed when I got home and asked God to show me what to do.

"This morning, I called Shaun and invited him to the game. He said he'd love to watch them play. He really wants to meet Jeremy. It was like God was making the way for everything to come together."

"Oh, it's gonna come together, all right," Gina predicted. "Ow! Katherine, stop hitting me when you don't like what comes out of my mouth."

"Then stop talking." She leaned forward in her seat as Abby made the turn. "Can I tell Nick he's coming?"

"No."

"Why not?" Both women asked.

Abby eased to a stop in a parking space in front of the florist's shop. "If you tell Nick, you know he's going to tell Jeremy. And then Jeremy is either going to call me or come to my office and yell at me for whatever reason, and then I'm going to yell at him and this time there won't be any taking the words back. I'll resign from the finance committee and change the projects I volunteer for at the church, so I don't have to be around him. I'm good with the fact that he isn't who or what God wants for me. With all I have going on right now, there isn't a lot of time for dating. God will show me who the right man is for me—at the right time. Besides, the only thing linking Jeremy and me together is church and our friendships with you and Nick."

Katherine was the first one out of the car. "I know this is hard for you. But if you know he's going to be upset, don't you think you should tell him?"

Abby set the car alarm before dropping her keys in her purse and reaching for the entrance door. Inside the shop, the air hung heavy with the perfume of sweet lilies and roses. "I'd rather wait and introduce them after the game."

"You want to introduce Jeremy to a former NBA star who was paid a fortune to do what these two amateur league teams do each weekend for free? I'll admit Nick and Jeremy are great players, but they're not NBA quality, and I think they'll both be embarrassed." Katherine smiled at the florist as he approached.

"Jeremy said he'd dreamed of playing in the NBA when he was a kid. I thought this would be a way for him to meet a real player."

The florist's greeting ended their discussion for a few minutes. But when the man went in search of the exact shade of turquoise ribbon for the bouquets, Katherine picked up where they left off. "Or Jeremy might take it as a reminder of what he isn't. Or, he could think it's a chance to meet the new man in your life."

Abby glared at her. "There is no man in my life."

One of the workers nearby gave them an interested look and sidled closer. Gina stepped into her path and chatted with her about a colorful bouquet half an aisle away.

Abby threw Gina a grateful smile, then lowered her voice when she said to Katherine, "We've attended a few social functions as friends, and we went to the movies that one time. Otherwise, we only share a meal when my parents are in town, and Daddy invites him to join us. So, no, there is no man in my life, especially not Jeremy. Shaun is only five years older than Jeremy, and he's nice. Besides, I find it a bit mercenary to ask the man for close to a million dollars without introducing him to the person whose dream he's making come true."

"So, you're the fairy godmother?" Gina rejoined the group just in time to insert one of her zingers. She gave Abby an impish grin while twisting one of her light brown curls around her finger.

"There is no fairy tale."

"Sure there is. Nick and Kat are the prince and princess. You helped get them together, and now you're going to grant Jeremy's wish. You're the fairy godmother."

Katherine waved a silk sunflower in the air as if it were a wand. "She has a point."

Abby threw her hands up in disgust. "This is ridiculous. I can't call Shaun and cancel. I already asked him to do this instead of coming to one of Jeremy's Tuesday night games with the youth."

"That would have been perfect. The boys would love the chance to meet him."

"I thought so, too. But when I told Jeremy, he went about as nuts over that as he did the interview idea. That's why I'm not telling him Shaun will be with me on Saturday." She turned back to Gina. "You had better not breathe a word of this to your reporter boyfriend. The last thing I need is a media circus. Jeremy would kill me."

"I'm not seeing Toby right now, so your secret is safe." Gina's usual perkiness was subdued.

With the ribbons matched to the swatches of fabric, Abby, Gina, and Katherine went in search of lunch. Gina grabbed the restaurant door and held it for them to go inside, out of the heat. Her stomach growled as Abby walked past, and she grinned. "Who knew wedding planning required this much work? I need some protein."

Abby laughed. "Should we ask if they have a triple-decker burger?"

"It wouldn't hurt," Gina said.

They chose an available booth in the corner near the television. The Hawks' game was on display over their heads in high definition.

"Tell him, don't tell him. This has to be your call. I'm just asking you to put yourself in Jeremy's place. How would you feel if he brought the First Lady to a luncheon where you were the guest speaker?" Katherine asked her after she'd scooted to the center of the L-shaped table.

Abby smiled when the hostess handed her a menu. "I would feel very inadequate."

"There's your answer."

"Well, it's too late now. I've invited him, and he's accepted. If you know a way to get Jeremy not to show up at their last game before play-offs, I'm all ears."

"Oh, no, you made this disaster. You arrange for the hazmat team."

Katherine's words, or the cloud of coming disaster they promised, dulled Abby's appetite, and she ended up with a small salad and a bowl of potato soup. Katherine cleaned her salad plate, even using the half of a dinner roll she allowed herself to sop up the sweet vinaigrette dressing. Gina somehow managed to avoid smearing mustard on anything made of cloth, but twice Abby discreetly motioned with her finger at Gina's chin where a dab of mayo or ketchup lingered.

After they had finished their meal and all piled back into Abby's car for the drive to Katherine's, a sense of calamity stayed with her. She waved goodbye to Gina and Kat before driving off. She had two contracts to review for a meeting Monday morning.

But insecurities about her invitation to Shaun to watch Jeremy's team play tormented her on Sunday and into the next week. She marked the days on the calendar with a sick sense of dread pooling in her stomach.

She continued to pray, trusting God to guide her. She didn't want to embarrass Jeremy. She had honestly thought he would enjoy meeting Shaun. He and Nick were two of the best players she'd watched. But admittedly, she wasn't a scout for the NBA. Was it wrong to pray for a snowstorm in late spring?

By Thursday, her nerves were nearly frayed in two. Then Shaun called her and canceled. His agent had booked him as a last minute fill-in for a charity game in Chicago. He promised to make it up to her, but she assured him it was fine and that they could talk when he got back.

Thank you, Jesus.

At Saturday's game, Jeremy was talking to Nick and Katherine when Abby joined them on the bleachers behind the players' bench. He made eye contact with her and gave her a genuine smile. If a smile and a "glad you're here" look could smooth out some of the sharp edges in their friendship, he was all for it.

Katherine spoke first. "Hey, I thought you were bringing your new friend."

Just like that, Jeremy's good intentions nosedived. "What friend?"

Abby glanced between him and Katherine with wide eyes, tugging at the hem of her Panthers shirt. "No, I'm solo today. Shaun's hosting a charity tournament in Chicago."

"Shaun, as in Shaun Fowler of the Hawks?" Nick asked, bringing himself into the conversation.

"He does a lot for charities. I've been working with him on raising the funds for the recreation center. He wanted to come watch you guys play. But, like I said, it will have to be another time."

Jeremy scowled. "Abby, I really don't think that's a good idea. He'll be a distraction to everyone and I'm sure he has better things to do with his time than watch a bunch of wannabe players that aren't fit to warm the Hawks' bench during the season. It would be embarrassing for both teams."

Abby's face paled. He cringed. His rebuke had come out harsher than he'd intended, but what was she thinking? Just imagining the number of paparazzi snapping pictures all over the place had him breaking out in a cold sweat. Marshal Dekker would have his hide.

Nick and Katherine remained silent. When Abby's eyes met his, Jeremy regretted every word that had come out of his mouth. He'd hurt her. Again.

She straightened her shoulders, and any outward sign that his words had affected her was gone. "Then I guess it worked out for the best. But you're going to have to give in on letting him visit one of your Tuesday-night sessions with the boys. He was very interested in those. They are one of the main reasons he's considering our proposal."

She had him there. Not just because they had witnesses, but also because the building was meant as an outreach to the kids in the community. If the man was willing to donate his money to their cause, Jeremy was wrong to allow his foolish pride or jealousy over Shaun's contact with Abby to stand in the way.

"Let me know what date is open on his schedule, and I'll make sure we have as many youth there to participate as I can round up. But still, no press, please."

The buzzer sounded, warning the players they had five minutes until tip-off. Jeremy didn't take his eyes off her until she nodded her agreement. Then he followed Nick back on to the court and got in a few practice shots before huddling up with the rest of the team and receiving last-minute advice from their coach.

To say Jeremy was off his game was the understatement of the year. She'd almost brought an NBA All-Star to watch him play amateur ball. Just thinking about the possibility had him missing every free throw and three-pointer he attempted.

Nick finally came up to him during a time-out and handed him a towel. "You're done, buddy. Let someone else have a chance at making the play."

Jeremy wiped the sweat off his face as he walked toward the team's bench. Nick's words summed up more than just the current game where he was underperforming. They also applied to Abby's hard work to raise the money for the center despite his lack of cooperation when she could have really used his support.

He needed perspective. Someone who could help him understand the situation better and help him see why his emotions were churning into a raging storm just waiting to explode. If he wanted to keep Abby as a friend, he needed to find a way to accept the rules over his life and balance them against what it meant to be her friend. Period.

As soon as the game was over, he turned down Nick's weekly offer to join Katherine and him for lunch. Abby had left just before the game ended, saving him from creating an excuse even he wouldn't believe. He slung his bag over his shoulder and walked to his car. He hadn't seen his parents in a couple of weeks, so this sudden visit wouldn't be a surprise.

"Well, look what the cat dragged in, Delores." Jeremy's father caught him in a bear hug and slapped him on the back. He let him into the house they'd been given fourteen years ago when they'd entered witness protection.

"Jeremy. Oh, it is so good to see you." His mother held his face in her hands and inspected him from head to toe. "You've lost weight. Have you been sick?" And automatically, the back of her hand was pressed against his forehead.

He ducked out of reach. "No, Mom, I don't have a fever. I'm not sick. I've just been busy."

"I tell your father all the time how much I worry about you. I don't know why you can't find a nice young lady and settle down. I'm sure your church members would feel more confident about your dedication to them if you had a wife. I've never heard of a minister waiting until he's thirty to start looking for a wife."

"Mom, stop. Just stop. You know I won't consider marriage until I can reclaim ownership of my life. Not until Dekker and his rule book are gone. I couldn't ask the woman I love to live her life under a microscope just because I have to."

She would have said more, but his father redirected her attention by rubbing his chest with the heel of his hand. "Cliff, is your chest paining you? Did you take your medicine? I laid it out for you."

"Yes, I took my medicine. I'm fine. Jeremy's fine. We're both fine. You, however, are working yourself into one of your panic attacks. Go enjoy a cup of that tea you drink when you get anxious. It will help you relax. I need to talk to Jeremy about man stuff."

She harrumphed but left them alone. His father led him into his equivalent of a man cave, a room with dark paneled walls, a big area rug and a huge leather recliner facing a giant high-definition television. Jeremy smiled. Maybe he'd inherited his need for a recliner and the largest television on the market, along with his tall, lean build, from his father.

After turning the volume down on the Braves game, his father motioned him to the leather sofa separated from the big recliner by a narrow end table. "So, I'm guessing there's a woman involved." Just like that, Cliff Walker wiped out all the superfluous details and left the heart of the matter standing, untouched.

"How—"

He raised his hand. "Your face is hanging so low

you look like you've lost your best friend. And when your mother hit you with her marriage complaint, your answer was direct instead of a dodge."

Jeremy blinked and slumped back into the cushions. How did he do that?

"And, even though I don't have an office anymore, I am an accountant. I know when things won't add up the second I look at them." He rested his arm on the side of his chair and leaned toward Jeremy. "And you, son, don't add up today."

"Good thing I'm a minister and would never try to lie to you. You'd catch me every time."

"I always did."

Jeremy's gaze went to his.

"Before you were a minister." His father grinned. "I enjoyed your sermon last week. It means a lot to your mother and me that we can listen to you preach on the radio. I didn't think Dekker and his pack were going to go for it when you suggested it. But I guess pointing out that anyone could video record the service and post it on YouTube helped him see reason."

"He isn't one to agree with much that isn't his idea. God answered our prayers on that one." Recovered from his shock at his dad's acuity, Jeremy grinned.

His dad reclined back in his chair, laced his fingers together and rested them across his stomach. "What's troubling you, son?"

Now that he was here, all the words and worries jumbled in his mind, and he didn't know where to begin. He closed his eyes and asked God to lead him. The image of Abby's face in the newspaper photo filled his mind. She was the heart of the matter, maybe even a piece of his heart, if he were totally honest with himself. But that was for another time.

"Do you remember my friend, Abby Blackmon?"

"That pretty woman whose father is a senator? You've talked about her often. In fact, when nothing happened with Katherine, I sort of thought you might think of her as more than a friend."

"No, we're just friends. And it will stay that way with any woman as long as Dekker's around. Dekker saw the picture of us in the paper. It didn't matter that they spelled my name wrong or that it only showed the back of my head. He called and chewed me out. He sees her as a risk. Never mind that she chairs the finance committee for the church and we're in the middle of building a recreation center. Her first idea was to have a bunch of newspaper and local news reporters interview me about the project. I refused because of Dekker. When I couldn't explain to her why, she got angry. And now she's found what she's calling the perfect solution."

"And that is?"

"Former NBA star Shaun Fowler."

His father let out a low whistle. "I've seen him play."

Jeremy grunted. "Yeah, me, too. Anyway, she's working with him, meeting him for dinner, moving right along as if my concerns about media exposure are nothing."

"Which concerns?"

He looked at his father. "You, Mom and me."

"You explained to her about Dekker?"

"I can't. Telling no one about our situation was

Dekker's second rule, right after keeping our faces out of the paper." Jeremy let out a long breath and leaned back.

"Let me tell you something about Marshal Dekker. He was overzealous as a new marshal when all this relocation stuff happened, and he's gotten used to barking orders and having them obeyed without question. But there are times people shouldn't blindly obey the rules and not ask questions. He doesn't know everything, and our relocation was a precautionary measure, not a requirement. I agreed to relocate because I thought it would create less stress for your mother. Darius's death came at a time when I wasn't sure if I would be around to protect my family, and leaving town cut down on the risk of danger for you and your mother."

"What? Are you telling me we didn't have to move? You dragged me away from all my friends and a chance to wow the scouts Kentucky had sent to watch me play on a freakish chance something *might* happen to us?" Fire, white and hot, surged through his veins. He thought he'd battled and won the war against the resentment that had almost consumed him over having his dream ripped from his hands. Before he'd had a chance to find out if he was good enough.

How many times had he stood in the pulpit, encouraging the congregation to let go of their bitterness and allow God to fill them with something better? Apparently, he was just as human as his flock. He ignored the shame tapping at his conscience.

"Don't take that tone with me, young man. I was protecting my family the best way I could at the time. Your mother and I prayed, and we prayed hard before making that decision. No, I didn't ask you because all you could see was the sparkle of a college championship trophy and dollar signs on the contract you would sign with the NBA. I saw a temptation that could lead you down a road you might not find your way back from. You had started hanging out with the wrong crowd, pushing curfew and getting a little mouthy with your mother and me because I wasn't well enough to stop you."

The anger zinging through him wouldn't let him stay still. Jeremy sprang to his feet. He paced off the length of the couch, trying to wrap his mind around his father's revelation. His churning emotions held on to the truth that they'd cheated him out of his dream. Guilt surged through him at the reminder of his rebellion against God and his parents when his father had been too weak to rein him in. It was like pouring gasoline on a fire. It flared higher, giving unnecessary fuel to his anger.

"How could you do that to me?"

"I did it because I loved you too much to watch you ruin your life."

"Ruin my life? I could have been a professional basketball player, earning millions of dollars." He stopped and stared at his father. Peaceful serenity surrounded the older man while streaks of lightning snapped and sparked around himself.

"I haven't heard a single word about God in the middle of your imagined glory and riches. Do you like your life, the way it is right now?"

"Right now? Not really. Because of the picture in the

paper, Dekker suggested I distance myself from some-one I'm just discovering I really like being with." He stopped and swallowed against the lump in his throat. "Her father's political position means she's lived her life in front of the camera. I've spent mine hiding in a dark corner. I believe with all my heart that this recreation center is an outreach ministry God wants us to use to reach more kids throughout Pemberly, but the restrictions on my life are slowing down the progress. Abby's found a way around my lack of cooperation, but it's put her in the path of a man who is living the life that should have been mine. The part that almost rips my heart out every day is she's convinced she's doing all this for me." His fist pounded against his chest. "So, no, I don't have anything to like about my life right now."

His father watched him and shook his head. "I'm sorry you're going through all this upheaval at one time. She must really care about you to still be trying to make your dream a reality after you shut her out."

"We're just friends. If she thought of me as anything more than that, she wouldn't have been so quick to go out with Mr. Superstar."

"Depends on how convincing you were when you told her you didn't want to be in the picture." His father chuckled. "Sorry, couldn't help it. But tell me this, if someone refused to go along with you on a plan that made perfect sense to you and refused to give you an explanation as to why, how long would you argue, trying to change their mind?"

"What?" Jeremy dropped down on the sofa. Resting his elbows on his knees, he held his head in his hands.

His dad sat beside him and gripped his shoulder. "Can you trust her not to reveal your secret?"

"It's against the rules."

"I know you're a minister and took all those classes at seminary on counseling, but trying to tell yourself what to do about this is as smart as a doctor trying to take out his own tonsils."

Jeremy's head whipped around, and he locked gazes with his father. "What do you think I need to do? She's the media darling of Pemberly, and I'm the Phantom of the Opera, living in the shadows, forbidden to even have a photo of the back of my head appear in the papers."

"Well, to start with, you need to get over yourself."

Had his father been comparing notes with Abby? And then the realization smacked him upside his hard head. When he hadn't paid attention to Abby's words, God had sent him to his father for the same lecture.

He let out a slow breath as that truth infused his heart. His anger receded like a sudden low tide, and serenity took its place. "I'm working on that."

"And the next thing you should do is get on your knees and ask God what you're supposed to do about *everything*. Then, do that."

"*Then, do that.* You make it sound like I'm working a jigsaw puzzle."

"You are. It's called your life, and it isn't even a drop in the ocean compared to the wonders and works of our Heavenly Father. One piece at a time." His father slid him a sly grin. "But you already knew that, didn't you?"

Chapter 3

Abby linked arms with Gina as they walked out of the sanctuary and into the April sunshine. "I need a big favor."

Gina slowed her pace and turned, giving her an impish grin. "If it involves me being anywhere near Shaun Fowler, I'm your girl."

"It does involve Shaun, but you can't act like some star-crazed groupie every time you're around him if you're going to help me."

Gina huffed at her criticism. "I can work with anyone no matter their looks, celebrity status, bank account balance or their looks." She waggled her eyebrows. "You did notice I mentioned hunkiness twice?" Her face relaxed into a more serious expression. "I'm very professional in whatever job I'm doing. I mean, my boss is marrying a city councilman."

Abby patted her arm. "I have full faith in you. But this is a big project, and we're starting from scratch without much time to work out the kinks before the contractor gets started. As it is, the rainy season will be here any time now, and that will delay the foundation work. I want this building finished and presented to the town by Christmas."

"Those are some lofty goals for someone who had to rework her whole finance plan just a few days ago. Why don't we grab some lunch while you tell me all about how you need my help handling six feet, nine inches of basketball yumminess."

They took Gina's car, leaving Abby's in the parking lot, and drove to Diane's All-Natural Delights. Bypassing the line of people waiting for a seat inside, they claimed a small table on the patio shaded from the sun by a huge burgundy umbrella. With iced teas placed in front of them, they gave the waiter their order.

"Okay, what's my role in this endeavor?" Gina rubbed her hands together then reached for one of the baked tortilla chips still warm from the oven, and dunked it into a bowl of the best fresh-made salsa in all of Pemberly.

Abby leaned in, making sure she had Gina's full attention. "Promise me that, whatever you learn or hear about Shaun, you won't share any of it with Toby. The last thing anyone needs is for him to use something he discovered through you in a feature article for the *Sentinel*."

Gina clicked her nails on the table with her mouth quirked to the side. "If you have such trouble trusting me, why do you want me helping you?"

"It's not that I don't trust you. I just have to be really careful working with someone at this level of celebrity. He has a PR firm that handles his publicity, and we could be sued if Toby decides to print something he learned from you, whether you told him or not. It isn't you that I don't trust, Gina. It's your boyfriend." She reached out and squeezed her hand for reassurance.

Gina moved the silverware around on her napkin, not meeting Abby's gaze. "I've already told you Toby and I are not an item. Besides that, I'm very careful about what I discuss in his presence. He's always looking for the big story that will make him famous. I'm not going to be the one who provides him with it. So you have nothing to worry about."

"I'm sorry. This whole Jeremy thing has me paranoid, and I'm trying to keep everything low-key, which is really hard with a sports celebrity as the face of the project."

The waiter arrived with their lunch. Gina removed the top piece of bread from her sandwich and made a nest of lettuce, tomato and pickles over the shaved ham before finishing it off with a circle of mustard from the squirt bottle the waiter had brought her. Abby sprinkled salt on her cantaloupe slices, careful not to get any on her watermelon. They both bowed their heads in silent but separate prayers.

Abby took a sip of tea to wet her suddenly dry throat. "My friend who put me in touch with Shaun cautioned me that he is a bit of a player." At Gina's quirked eyebrow, she added, "Not like that. He really is nice. But while we were in the restaurant the last time, several photographers were trying to take our picture as we entered and exited the building. The church's efforts to do something great for Pemberly's youth shouldn't be turned into a media circus. And if the gossip columns start speculating on how many dinners we're having, whatever they say is a reflection on the church, my father and me. And I'd rather not be labeled Shaun Fowler's next flavor of the month."

Gina paused in the act of taking a bite of her sandwich. "I was kidding about the marrying him thing. It would be cool to meet him and even be able to tell my grandkids, if I ever have any, that I worked with him back in the day. But I don't want a picture of us in the paper under the headline, 'Fowler goes for plain vanilla legal assistant in a rebound,' either."

Abby slapped her napkin over her nose and mouth. The lemon from her tea burned her nasal passages, but she stopped it from spewing across the table. When she was able to talk again, she said, "Then you understand my position. I have to meet with him several times a month. And since I have a day job and my work with the finance committee has to be done after hours, the only times I have available are the evenings I'm not doing something for the church.

"I'm not comfortable going to his place or inviting him to mine. My apartment is connected to my parents' house, and I park in their garage and use their kitchen. But they're in Washington so much, it's like I have this monster of a house all to myself. Nothing would ever happen if Shaun came there. I'm not interested in him that way. But I don't want to give anyone something to talk about. Restaurants have been the best solution, even though they expose the frequency of our meetings to the media."

Gina scrunched her nose. "As great as Katherine is at being flexible with my schedule, I don't think she'll be too hip on me taking extended lunches to meet with a hunky, famous sports star. She loves me, but somehow, because it's me, she won't buy that it's all 'church business,' if you know what I mean."

"She trusts you completely—just like I do. So that isn't even an issue. But lunches would be a problem with the distance." Abby sat back after popping a chunk of cantaloupe into her mouth and chewing.

"So, what do you have in mind?"

"How about if we share him?"

Gina's fork hit her plate with a clatter. "Excuse me?"

"My meetings with Shaun are strictly business, but I don't want to offend him because, well, there isn't anything wrong with him. He's handsome, well spoken, and he's been a perfect gentleman at our dinners and on the phone. But this is just business. He doesn't do anything for me on a romantic level. The recreation center is too important to risk alienating our biggest sponsor. And I have no idea what he expects. He asked me why I'm always available for dinner on such short notice. I told him I have a very flexible schedule, but I know he's going to ask if I'm seeing anyone. I won't lie to him, but I also don't want to encourage him."

Gina wiped her mouth before laying her napkin next to her plate. "What can I do?"

Abby rubbed her temple where a pulsing throb was

increasing to jackhammer levels. She met Gina's inquisitive gaze with a serious one. "I would like you to assist me on the fund-raising campaign and come with me whenever I have to meet with Shaun. You can help me keep track of the contractor's progress and the paperwork between the bank, the permits office and the architect."

Gina cocked her head to the side while studying her. "You don't think Shaun will have a problem with me tagging along as a third wheel?"

"You won't be a third wheel. When we meet next week for dinner, which I expect you to attend with me, I'll explain how big this project is for us. I'm bringing you on board to help me. And you need to be kept in the loop so you're able to step in whenever I'm unavailable."

"I'm not actively on the finance committee."

"I know. But you're Katherine's assistant. Nick's on the committee, and he's marrying Katherine in two months."

"This will be the first job I ever got through associated nepotism." She grinned. "Well, I said I was your girl and I am. I will have a short, almost unnoticeable fan girl moment, and then I'll be good to go by the time they serve the entrée."

Abby watched her, waiting for another pithy comment. Instead, she held one hand over her heart and raised the other as if she was pledging an oath. "Scout's honor, even though those mean girls kicked me out after the first cookie campaign."

Abby's jaw dropped, but Gina just shrugged. "I ate

more cookies than I sold. My parents made me dip into my piggy bank to pay off my debt. I still have to close my eyes when I walk past their little table outside the grocery store. Thank goodness they don't have their phones set up to accept debit cards. I'd be as big as the side of a barn."

As soon as she caught her breath and her eyes stopped watering from her laughter, Abby brought Gina up to speed on the project. She gave her a packet with the schedule of meetings with not only Shaun but also the finance committee, the contractor and the bank.

When Gina dropped her back at the church, Jeremy's car was parked under a big oak tree. He was probably reviewing his sermon for the evening service. Or maybe he'd gone to lunch with a church member and hadn't made it back yet. The urge to walk toward the entrance to the church office, to go inside and lay out the new plans on his desk was almost irresistible, but she won the battle.

She drove home with her heart heavy with the truth that she didn't feel as welcome to barge into his office unannounced as she had a month ago. The uncertainty of the state of their friendship was a cold, hollow ache near her heart. She missed him.

Jeremy glanced toward Abby's red Lexus still sitting in the parking lot. Katherine had dropped Nick and him off in front of the church office after their lunch at Maida's Cafe. He didn't know if the jolt in his chest at seeing her car was the quickening of hope at finding her inside or the dread of having to face her, knowing how unkind his last words to her had been.

The friction between them left him worried about the survival of their friendship. But despite the restrictions on his life, if friendship was all he could claim with Abby, he would cherish every moment. He missed his friend.

Nick's voice dragged him back from his inner musings. "She isn't here. I saw her leave with Gina while we were waiting for you."

Jeremy let out a deep sigh. "Yeah, she doesn't really have anything to talk to me about."

"What's going on between you two?" Nick held the door to the hall open so Jeremy could go ahead of him and unlock his private office.

"Nothing. We're good."

Following him inside, Nick took a seat facing his desk. He waited until Jeremy settled into his leather chair and they were eye to eye. "Uh-huh. That claim might fly with your staff, but I saw the disgusted look on your face after you unloaded on her about Shaun Fowler yesterday. And you were anything but 'good' on the court during the game. So, you can either tell me, or I'll sweet-talk it out of Kat. And you know she's going to take Abby's side and paint you as the big bad wolf in the story. I'd like to hear your version, so I can at least defend you."

He blew off Nick's words as if they weren't the brutal truth. "It's nothing. She went all gaga over Shaun, and I felt the need to caution her about being taken in by all the flash and attention his celebrity status will bring to their relationship."

"Relationship? Hold on a second. Are you saying Abby's dating this guy? Dude, what happened to you asking her over for a quiet dinner with Kat and me?"

Jeremy met Nick's confused gaze with resignation to the emptiness that was his life. "Abby deserves a man who can give her the world. One who is her equal when it comes to social and financial status. The press hasn't painted too bad a picture of Shaun. But I still think he's a ladies' man. I don't want her getting in over her head."

"So, you're her big brother now? Just looking out for her best interests instead of trying to turn her interest toward you?"

Jeremy looked away. "I'm not the guy for Abby. I never was. I can't give her the things she needs."

Nick leaned back and folded his arms across his chest. "Did she say that, or did something happen to you overnight that made you too chicken to even try?"

He was on his feet, leaning across the desk ready to snatch Nick out of his chair, before reality froze him in midsnarl. He closed his eyes and prayed, asking for peace and wisdom to guide him through this conversational minefield. Easing out a slow breath, he pulled back. "There are things about my life I can't explain. It doesn't mean I'm a coward. It just means I know Abby's and my relationship is best left as is. That way I don't let her down, and neither of us thinks there's more than there can ever be."

"And you buy that garbage you're spouting out of your mouth? Come on, Jeremy. I'm your friend. I saw the look on your face when you realized you hurt her yesterday. You were there for Kat and me when I was trying to show her how important she was to me and I was making a total mess of things. You told me we only hurt the ones we love. You had all the makings of a lovesick puppy yesterday."

Jeremy hadn't invited Nick back to the church office so he could give him the third degree. He wanted his opinion on a camp that Stuart Wise, the youth minister, was proposing as the location for next year's summer mission trip. And now was the time to start that conversation and get Nick off his back.

Nick's job on the finance committee was to oversee the expenses for the youth department, including their mission trips. Jeremy slid the brochures over to him. The camp was in North Carolina and perfect for the older teens' summer retreat. The place was huge and very popular. They needed to get their deposit in soon or the camp would be sold out.

Nick glanced at the papers and nodded. They each flipped through an identical packet, pausing to discuss the pricing on a few of the activities and the deadline for paying the deposit.

"Would you rather the parents pay the church and we write one check for each phase of the payment plan, or do you want them to mail their checks directly to the camp?" Jeremy asked.

"Have Stuart find out how many parents are onboard with the cost and distance. We can cut them one check from the church. We'll keep track of who pays and when. But let Stu know we'll cover the cost for any of the families who might run into a financial snag, so their kids don't have to miss out."

"Will you use the scholarship fund to cover any shortfalls?"

Nick shook his head. "No, I went to this camp with my cousin one summer. It was a lot of fun. We went into the surrounding areas doing work for the elderly around their homes that they couldn't do themselves. We hosted bonfires at night with hot dogs and s'mores to attract the local kids. It's a poor area despite the size and quality of the camp, so there's a great need for lending a hand. If any of the kids have a problem paying their way, I'll cover their registration fees."

Jeremy sat back, studying his friend. "Katherine is definitely having a positive effect on you."

"It doesn't have anything to do with Kat." He grinned. "Well, it might. If she found out I was donating money toward registration, she'd just tell me to pay for all of them, so it's fair to everyone."

They both laughed. "I had to hide the receipts for the cruise I booked for our honeymoon. She'd have us staying home and donating the money to the missionaries in other countries." Nick held up his hand. "Don't get me wrong. I would be fine with that if she would agree to actually stay home for those two weeks, but she'd have us out volunteering at whatever charity needed a hand or visiting some of the kids from her case files. I love that woman and her giving heart, but the only way I can make her stop and relax is by marooning her aboard a ship in the middle of the ocean with no cell phone access. And then I'll have to keep her out of the internet cafe."

Nick's cell phone chimed, halting their laughter. He

checked the message before glancing back at Jeremy. "That was Kat. She's on her way back with Radar. We're taking him for a run in the dog park. Are we good here about the summer camp?"

"I'll have Stuart book it tomorrow."

Nick stood up. "And you aren't going to tell me anything else about the situation with Abby either, are you?"

"There isn't anything to tell because there isn't a situation. Abby is working with Shaun Fowler and I'm doing other things." When Nick turned back, Jeremy clapped him on the shoulder, urging him out of the office. He walked with him down the hall and through to the glass doors that led to the covered portico where Katherine waited. A young dog was yipping and bouncing up and down in the passenger seat.

Nick opened the car door while Katherine wrestled with the puppy to keep him from escaping. Jeremy watched as Nick leaned over and bussed her on the cheek. They both waved to him as they drove off.

An ache of longing rushed through him at their sweet display of affection. They would have forever to enjoy being together, the same way he knew he'd never have the opportunity to share that kind of joy. They deserved every moment of happiness they found with each other. God had blessed them well. He glanced across the parking lot. Abby's car was gone.

He stood beside the church, his lone shadow cast against the wall of the house of worship. He went inside to review that night's sermon and do some soul searching that could only happen through prayer. Perhaps God would give him a sign that everything was going according to His plan. Because Jeremy was positive, nothing was going the way *he* thought it should.

Chapter 4

Abby tapped her pen against the blotter on her desk, staring at the phone as if it were a spitting kitten ready to claw her if she reached out to touch it. They were three weeks into the new fund-raising plan involving Shaun Fowler. The church bookkeeper had turned over the financial information Gina had requested. The application was complete.

It had been waiting on her desk when she came in this morning. Gina had done her part; now it was up to Abby. She let out a muted hiss and rubbed her forehead where a dull ache had begun. "This is ridiculous. I'm ridiculous."

Gina popped her head inside her office. "Uh, did you know I was out here, or are you talking to yourself again?"

"What?" Abby glanced up, taking a second to let Gina's question penetrate the fog of self-doubt covering her every action this morning. She tried to smile. "Yes and yes. I heard you opening and closing file drawers out there. Which reminds me, thank you again for rescuing me when my assistant's doctor put her on immediate bed rest and then her replacement quit the temp agency after only one day." She heaved a long sigh and confessed. "Actually, I was giving myself a pep talk to overcome my sudden lack of communication skills where Jeremy is concerned."

Gina's need to be in the middle of everything was the stuff of legend. Abby shook her head when Gina strolled into the office and sat down across from her. If she could get away with it, Abby would hand over the entire recreation center project to her to put an end to the discomfort holding her friendship with Jeremy hostage. But that wasn't the answer.

Abby had never shirked her responsibilities, no matter how unpleasant the task, and she wasn't starting now. Even at the risk of losing Jeremy as a friend. She wouldn't ask someone to do something she wouldn't do herself. Something deep inside held her to her beliefs. She was doing her job, and that involved making Jeremy's dream happen, and the most important accomplishment of this project was reaching more of the community for God. There was no nobler purpose. She'd deal with Jeremy one encounter at a time.

"You don't have to call him. I'm happy to take the papers by the church office and have him sign them there. I'm the one who has to witness both signatures to notarize the forms for the bank. You can skip this part."

Katherine had warned her about Gina's uncanny ability to know what she was thinking. But Abby had thought it would take Gina longer to figure *her* out. She reached across the desk and squeezed Gina's hand. "Thanks, but I won't avoid him just because he has an issue with my fund-raising efforts. Efforts that are working, by the way."

Gina rolled her shoulders in the semblance of a shrug, then cast her gaze toward the phone. "Well?"

Any appreciation for the empathy evaporated, and Abby narrowed her gaze. "Fine." She snatched up the handset and punched in the number for Grace Community.

While she waited for Mrs. Hall to put her through, Gina settled into her chair. She cupped her chin in her palm and propped her elbow on the desk, as if waiting for the main event. If they had a microwave, she probably would have popped popcorn in readiness for the show.

"Abby?" Jeremy sounded surprised.

"Jeremy, listen, the loan papers are complete. But both Shaun and your signatures have to be notarized. Gina's working at my office all day today. I'd really appreciate it if you would stop by and sign them, so we can continue moving forward."

"My afternoon is clear. Would three o'clock work?"

"Perfect. I'll let Gina know to expect you." Without waiting for him to respond, she said goodbye and put the phone back in its cradle.

Gina straightened. "Well, that was definitely short and not so sweet."

"That was a business request. I was being professional."

Looping one of her curls around her finger, Gina shrugged. The phone rang, and Abby reached for the handset as she glanced at the caller ID. Jeremy. Terrific.

She forced her lips to curve into a smile. "Jeremy, is something wrong?" She didn't need to look at Gina to know she would be leaning in, trying to hear what he was saying. Some things were a given.

"You hung up before I could ask if Shaun would be there."

"I don't know yet. He's my next call. Why? Are you refusing to come if he's here?"

"No! I didn't say that. I just…"

"You just what?" She didn't give him a chance to answer. "I've had enough of your ostrich-like, head-buried-in-the-sand avoidance over a ministry that benefits the whole community. After you finish with Gina today, you and I are going to sit down and work out some of these issues, so I don't feel like I'm walking on eggshells while managing this project."

"Abby, I…" He heaved a deep sigh. "I would be happy to talk to you then."

Jeremy stared at the phone in his hand, the dial tone marking the end of another awkward conversation with Abby. He said a prayer for wisdom as he keyed in a number he knew by heart but wished he didn't.

"Dekker."

"Marshal Dekker, Jeremy Walker here." He drew a deep breath and followed his father's example by going straight to the heart of the matter. "We need to find a realistic way to handle my media exposure risk."

The man's gravelly laugh grated on Jeremy's already taut nerves. "Walker, you aren't thinking about making the news, are you? Got a big event where you need to serve as Miss Blackmon's escort?"

"No parties, Dekker. But since I followed one of *your* rules and refused to publicly promote building the recreation center the church is rallying the public to support, Abby won't be the only celebrity in Pemberly."

"Did you tell her about your situation?"

Jeremy gritted his teeth, resisting the urge to tap the headset against his forehead. "No. That's against the rules, too. I told Abby she would have to find a way to raise the money that didn't include my doing public interviews."

"If she found another way, what's the problem?"

"Number one, I'm the pastor of the church funding the project. My lack of support is raising questions with a local newspaper reporter. Number two, since I was the one pushing so hard for this and now I've taken myself out of the process without being able to explain why, Abby has recruited Shaun Fowler and his Sports for Kids organization to help draw attention to our need. Plus, he's donating over half the money for the project."

Finally, Jeremy had the marshal's attention, judging by the long pause on the other end of the line.

"Shaun Fowler, the retired NBA star?"

"Yep! So, if you thought having my picture in the

paper was a problem, tell me how you plan to handle crowd control when Mr. Fowler shows up in Pemberly—at my church—with the paparazzi following in his wake."

"Can you stop them?"

"Stop who?" Jeremy railed into the phone. "Fowler or Abby? Because if I told Abby the truth, she'd do everything in her power to help me. But since you laid down your edict and I have no choice but to comply, I can't tell her anything but 'no,' so the only problem she is aware of is me." He pounded his fist against the center of his desk, scattering pens and pencils everywhere.

"You need to stop her. Tell her as little as you can about why, but convince her to find another way to raise the funds."

Jeremy's laugh was as bitter as the resentment trying to claw its way into his heart. "If I tell her any less, we won't be speaking to each other. Which is about where we're at right now, thanks to your rules. You have held this situation over my head and manipulated me into doing what you wanted for the past fourteen years. It's time you figured out how to solve a real-life problem with your hands tied behind your back for a change. I'm through hiding in the shadows waiting for the boogey man to find me—when he doesn't even exist. My father told me ours isn't a true WITSEC placement. You relocated us, but we didn't have to change our identities and there isn't anyone out to get us."

"Your father had just had a massive heart attack. His business partner waited until he was out on sick leave to cook the books for a crime family. If any of those people thought your father was the one who gave us those documents, someone would have been after all of you. And we wouldn't be having this conversation because you'd all be dead." His breath heaved in Jeremy's ear. "Listen, Pastor, the precautions I've asked you to take over the years have been to protect your parents. I know it can be tough having to stay focused on privacy—"

Jeremy's grip on the phone was so tight his fingers were going numb. "I wasn't even seventeen when all that happened. And focused on privacy? Dekker, do you like baseball?"

"What does baseball have to do with anything?"

"Answer. The. Question." Jeremy's jaw barely moved as he formed the words.

"Yeah, I catch a Braves game when I can. So?"

"Ever watched them play at the stadium?"

"Sure. I took my nephew to a game last month for his birthday. I still don't—"

"I've been to one live game. One. Do you know why?" He barreled forward without waiting. "I was with a friend sitting behind the Braves dugout. In the middle of the game, a foul ball popped back over us. The guy three rows up caught it. After the excitement in our section settled down, I looked up at the jumbotron to watch the replay of the man's catch. The camera had swept the section, starting with our row. I know because I recognized the design on the back of the shirt I was wearing. So, just trying to do something any normal, red-blooded American would do, I almost had my face plastered on national television because the camera kept panning our section while the coach was on the field talking to the pitcher. The only reason I wasn't in any more screen shots is because I was far enough away from the guy who caught the ball."

After a low whistle, Dekker cleared his throat. "I'm sorry about that, Jeremy. WITSEC is always a new life, a new start for the participants, and our job is to keep them safe. Your family's situation is unique. Maybe we should have sat down and discussed a better way to allow you a higher quality of life that didn't make you feel like you had to hide from the world. But that's why people go into witness protection. To save their lives."

The marshal's confession cooled some of the heat in Jeremy's anger. It didn't offer a solution to his problem, though. He still couldn't share his secret with Abby, and he still couldn't be a visible part of her life where the media was concerned. He let out a weary sigh and checked his watch. "Dekker, I have an appointment to sign the loan papers linking me and Grace Community with Shaun Fowler and his organization. If you come up with a plan to give me my life back before we finish building the center, I'm all ears."

"Jeremy." Dekker's voice lowered. "Don't get your hopes up. These are the rules we expect everyone to go by. If we make an exception for you, others will come up with their idea of a unique situation. The program can't be personalized for each case."

"Yeah, I know. That's why I'm praying for a solution. God's rules make more sense, and they're easier to follow." After he hung up the phone, Jeremy reached into his middle desk drawer and pulled out his keys.

Signing the application was going to create a whole other set of risks for exposure. He tossed his keys in the air and caught them as he walked out the door. His lips twisted into a grim smile. He was just doing his part to provide Dekker with job security.

Abby stopped short just outside her office. The hallway echoed with the warm familiarity of a teasing male voice mingled with Gina's easy laughter. The joviality was coming from the office Gina used when she was either working on the recreation center project or as Abby's temporary legal assistant.

Tugging her suit jacket firmly in place, Abby took a deep breath and tapped her knuckle against the half-open door. Gina and Jeremy looked toward her, their smiles frozen in place.

"I had no idea you had company, Gina." And not letting herself be a coward, she met Jeremy's gaze directly. "Or that you would arrive early."

Jeremy rose from his chair. His dimpled smile gone. "I didn't know how soon you needed the paperwork signed, and I didn't want to be accused of dragging my feet."

Her cheeks prickled with heat at the reference to his lack of cooperation. "Thank you for that. Shaun is tied up in meetings in his office outside Atlanta until late today. He invited Gina and me to dinner so he can sign them tonight. Then everything will go to the bank tomorrow."

There was a throat clearing from the doorway. Toby Hendricks, a reporter for the *Sentinel*, stood waiting to be invited in. "Don't mind me. I was hoping to catch Gina for a second."

Gina tapped a stack of papers against her desk, straightening them. "Jeremy and I were just visiting. I'm through with him." She met Abby's gaze with an impish grin. "He's all yours."

Abby's response was nonverbal. But her squinted glare spoke for itself. She looked at Jeremy. "Then I guess it's my turn at him. We can speak in my office."

Jeremy stood, offering the other man his chair. Toby nodded and started forward. A quick glance at Gina had Abby concerned. Gone was her previous cheeky confidence, replaced with a lip-gnawing nervousness. Was it so wrong for Abby to enjoy seeing Gina squirm for once?

Toby offered his hand to Jeremy in greeting. "Pastor Walker, I guess the rumors are true about the church partnering with Shaun Fowler's Sports for Kids organization to build a recreation center here in Pemberly. Any chance I can interview you on what it's like working with a pro athlete for our feature story?"

Any warmth that had shown in Jeremy's demeanor vanished. Abby watched, stunned, as his muscles tensed until his shoulders were as rigid as wood planks underneath the expanse of fabric covering his back. He cut his eyes toward her, and the grim set of his jaw told her she would have one more example of noncooperation to add to the already long list of complaints against his behavior.

"Sorry, I'm taking a backseat on this project. Abby

and Gina are working with Shaun to make this project happen."

"Yeah, but—"

"I won't be granting any interviews. Talk to Abby or Shaun." With that, Jeremy turned and went to the door, waiting for Abby to precede him out of the room.

As soon as the door clicked shut behind them in her office, she spun to face him. "I cannot believe you just did that." She smacked the file folder in her hand down on the desk as if swatting a fly, then dropped into her chair.

Jeremy drew in a deep breath, pulling the fabric of his blue-and-yellow striped polo taut over his torso. "If I'd agreed to an interview, you would still be glaring at me, ready to throw something at my head. I'm just being consistent."

"Consistently difficult."

"Abby, there are tangible reasons I can't do an interview." And before she could go after him to name those reasons, he held up a hand. "But I can't tell you what they are, so don't ask."

She wasn't sure which was worse—the thumping pain in the middle of her forehead or the burning ache in her chest. For some reason he had the ability to make both areas throb in discomfort at the same time.

But she wasn't letting him off that easily. She motioned him to the chair facing her desk. "What *can* you tell me?"

He met her gaze with a determined one of his own. "As I've stated several times already, I'm not doing any interviews. If I answer Toby's questions, I'm only inviting more questions and attention, when I need to remove myself from direct association with this project."

Abby pressed her palms down on her desk, pushing up from her chair, and leaned toward him. "You know, that answer is as noncommittal and full of nothing as any politician's press secretary could recite. And it explains nothing. How about you tell me the truth for once? I promise whatever you say won't leave this room."

She watched him for any break in the set of his stubborn features. Nothing. She would have shaken him until he saw reason if she could. How could he sit there, looking at her with all the warmth gone from his eyes, knowing she was doing everything in her power to give him what he'd said was his dream?

She came around her desk and took the seat beside his, reaching a hand out and placing it over his where it gripped the narrow armrest. "Forget Shaun Fowler, the interviews and the recreation center. It's just you and me here. I know you have to have a strong reason for refusing to be interviewed. And I know you believe this new ministry is what God wants the church to do. I can help you. I want to help you. Just tell me what's holding you back, so we can fix it."

At her heartfelt plea, his expression shifted. She'd never beheld a more tortured visage. He wouldn't meet her gaze.

She squeezed his hand again. "Please."

He reared up from his seat, his chair scooting back several inches. He drove his hands through his hair, then swung back to glare at her. His anger was a palpable being, pulsing between them. "Don't you think I want to? I can't."

She was done with compassion for him. If he wouldn't give her anything to work with, then he needed to understand theirs was nothing but a business relationship. "You win. That was the last time I'll beg you to share something with me that you won't."

"Can't."

"Does it matter which? Either way, you've shut me out." She straightened in her chair. "It's more appropriate for you to initiate contact with Shaun, since he's funding *your* ministry mission." She took a sticky pad from her desk and wrote down Shaun's cell and office numbers. She didn't stand up, just held the yellow paper out to him. "I expect you to call him this week. Thank him for his support, his interest in our project and for helping me make it a reality. The rest of what you say to him is up to you."

He reached for the paper. She held on to it. "But do not ever act like my big brother, father or someone I have anything but a professional relationship with again. You are not my keeper."

Jeremy snatched the paper from her fingers. "Afraid I'll mess up your chances with the superstar?"

She rose from her seat with the dignity of a queen reigning on high and moved to the door. She held it open, her eyes dry and her gaze directed at him as he walked toward her.

"Abby—"

"We're done. I'll have a full progress report ready for

the committee meeting next week. Expect an emailed copy the day before for your review. If you have any questions, feel free to call me here at the office."

He paused beside her in the doorway. "Abby."

She offered him nothing, just as he'd offered her. "Goodbye, Pastor Walker." She closed the door and leaned against it, biting her fist to keep the keening wail locked inside her throat. He'd never have a hint of proof as to how deep his silence cut into her soul. Never.

After Abby's chilly dismissal from her office, Jeremy walked outside into the warm spring sunshine. Toby Hendricks was sitting on the hood of his car. Great. All he needed was for Toby to whip out his phone and start snapping photos to use in his article for the paper. He needed to find an island where he could live as a hermit. But with the way his life was going right now, some rich developer would come in and build ocean-view condos for the rich and famous. And have a special hotel to house the hundreds of paparazzi that constantly followed them.

"Hendricks, I thought I explained that Abby is taking the lead on the rec center project."

"Oh, you did. I'm just curious as to why."

Jeremy hissed out a hot, slow breath, trying to take the edge off his temper. How many people did he have to say "no comment" to before they understood he meant it? "I don't have anything else to add. Abby will report to the finance committee, and I'll learn about her progress when the rest of the committee members do next week."

Toby scooted forward off the vehicle. "Yeah, that's what Gina told me. But I was wondering how you feel about Ms. Blackmon and Gina spending so much time with Shaun Fowler? I mean, the sports news has him pegged as a bit of a ladies' man, if you know what I mean."

If Jeremy ground his teeth together any harder, he'd need to make an appointment to be fitted for a pair of dentures. "Shaun Fowler is an NBA All-Star, a philanthropist who has taken an interest in Grace Community's efforts to provide a safe place for all of Pemberly's youth and he's single. Abby and Gina are both single, adult women fully capable of making their own decisions and knowing what they want. The last I heard, Shaun was more than pleased to be working with them. That should say it all."

"Can I quote you on that?" Toby smirked as he waved his phone in the air with the large speaker icon showing on the display.

Jeremy stepped forward. But instead of drawing on the well of anger bubbling high into the back of his throat, he closed his eyes and called on a power far stronger than his own. Peace settled over him, and his shoulders relaxed, his balled fists loosened.

"Toby, I'm going to give you a piece of advice. If you aren't in a committed relationship with Gina, you have no say over what she does any more than she has over what you do. Abby is the head of the finance committee at Grace Community Church. She is the most qualified person to bring this outreach mission to the community. Our church has prayed, I've prayed and our committee has prayed for God's guidance in all the actions we've taken regarding this project. We are following His lead." At Toby's scoffing eye roll, Jeremy smiled. "You might give it a try. His directions won't ever steer you wrong."

Jeremy pressed the button to unlock his car door, then climbed inside. Toby saluted before sauntering off toward his own vehicle. The sun was starting the gradual decline that marked late afternoon. The warmth of the spring day was slipping away just like the sun behind the clouds.

A chill ran along his collar and down across his chest where his seat belt rested over his heart. But this coldness wasn't on the outside where a jacket could chase it away. This loss of warmth was internal, delving down into the darkest reaches of his heart. Where he'd nurtured an even more impossible desire for something— someone—than living a normal life that didn't involve avoiding cameras.

The empty coldness of losing Abby's favor.

He'd dreamed of college superstardom that would have led to a first-round draft pick in the NBA. Which would have brought fame and fortune. He was ashamed that he'd wanted those things, craved them, even. But he'd been a clueless kid, chafing under the strictures of parents who expected him to make a difference for the good in this world. God had used Katherine and all she hadn't had growing up to open his eyes to just how blessed he was to be sitting in that classroom at the local junior college. That truth had sent him down another path. A path of thanksgiving and wanting to help others.

And the irony was that for all the good this recreation center would do for the people of Pemberly, it was going to dig the cavern separating him from Abby even deeper. He leaned his head back against the headrest in his car.

Ask and it shall be given unto you. Seek and ye shall find. Knock and it shall be opened unto you.

How many times had he encouraged church members to do those very things, assuring them that if they would truly believe, God would give them the deepest desires of their hearts?

He still believed. So he prayed there in the car, asking God to do just that. He understood that sometimes God took him through something difficult to prepare him to receive what was waiting for him. But, if he asked and believed, trusting in God, he would receive what was the very best for him.

And therein lay his fear. Abby was the best. She was so good and kind, and so strong in her faith. She would be a gift with a price worth more than rubies or gold or even diamonds. But was she what was best for him? Or still, was he what was best for her? Or was Shaun Fowler?

If it was Shaun, Jeremy prayed God would give him the strength to let go of his dreams of a future with her. It tore at the edges of his heart, tightening his chest with the fear of losing her. He stood in the pulpit every Sunday pleading with his congregation to take a leap of faith. To trust God's wisdom to give them what they needed.

He closed his eyes, willing his breathing to slow. It was time he did what he asked others to do. Abby and Gina were meeting with Shaun. If Abby made a personal connection with Shaun, he had no doubt she could handle the situation. She would seek God's guidance before starting a relationship with any man. Had she ever asked God about a relationship with him?

Chapter 5

"Hey, Pastor Walker," called a youth whose voice hadn't fully settled into the deeper bass of his larger midteen body. "What's the big surprise?"

Jeremy pulled the door lever on the smaller church bus inward. The doors swished together, sealing in the noise and rowdiness of a dozen teenage boys ranging in age from thirteen to seventeen. He checked a blur of motion in the overhead mirror as a teen sporting a lime-green T-shirt switched seats.

They were a motley crew, stretching from the slam-dunk-challenged height of five-five up to the too lean, rim-grabbing height of six-one. They were good boys, but if they had any clue what he'd lined up for them today, he'd never get them calmed down.

"By definition, a surprise is a surprise. Wait for it."

A dozen echoing groans expressed their impatience. He grinned. Some things about youth were universal. He hit Play on the sound system, and one of the popular Christian groups thumped out their latest hit. The boys settled down in their seats, and they were on their way.

Jeremy had done what he should have done without a reminder from Abby. He'd called Shaun and thanked him for his interest and the financial support for their recreation center. He was a nice guy. Jeremy could probably grow to like him if Abby wasn't the link between them.

Shaun was spending the day at one of the centers his foundation had helped build just outside Atlanta. He'd invited Jeremy to bring the teens to one of their weekly tournaments that included a group pizza party afterwards. When Jeremy had hesitated at the offer, Shaun informed him this was a routine occurrence at the center and not a media opportunity.

Abby must have mentioned his camera avoidance issues. If that got around to the congregation, the elders of the church would start slipping him therapists' business cards as they shook his hand on the way out after services. He let out a disgusted groan. He had no choice but to use his dislike of having his picture taken as the excuse it provided him to not be interviewed or photographed. How else could he explain what had him diving for cover to avoid any oncoming photo ops as if someone had tossed a live hand grenade into his path? God was keeping him humble.

Nick was joining them there after he finished meeting with a client. Jeremy needed someone to help keep the boys from acting like, well, teenagers, once they realized they were meeting an NBA basketball star. One of the kids was even wearing a Fowler jersey. That was a photo op just waiting to be caught. And Jeremy would make sure he was the one taking the picture. There was no better way to avoid being in front of the camera than being behind it.

Jeremy checked his watch and shook his head. Even driving just under the speed limit, they'd arrived forty minutes early. The outings with the boys never required as many bathroom breaks as the ones with the coeds did. The boys didn't push and shove too much as they exited the bus. Thanks, in part, to their not knowing what "surprise" was waiting for them. Stan, the Shaun-jersey fan, brought up the rear.

"Hey, Stan, did you bring a regular T-shirt?"

The lanky high school freshman paused on the last step and looked down at his chest. "Did I spill something on this one?"

Jeremy shook his head. "No, you're fine. I just wanted to know if you had a spare in case you ended up wanting to change."

When they recognized the man walking toward them in basketball shorts and a matching jersey, the hum of voices in the parking lot grew louder. The boys' horsing around shifted to surging excitement. He was bouncing a basketball in time to his steps as he drew closer.

"Shaun Fowler. It's Shaun Fowler. We're meeting Shaun Fowler!"

Their words became a buzzing chant building exponentially like the cicadas in the trees during the hot summer afternoons. The sound winged its way back to where Stan stood on that last step in the bus, his foot hovering above the pavement. He turned toward Jeremy, his eyes wide and sparkling with happy disbelief. Jeremy handed him a Sharpie.

"Go for it. I brought a few extra shirts in case any of you wanted him to sign what you're wearing instead of one of the posters they're giving out later."

It took Stan less than the blink of an eye to grab the marker, exit the bus and disappear into the group of boys flocking around the famous athlete. Jeremy had been just like them at that age. Full of awe over the pro players and their skills. His high school coach had encouraged him, comparing his abilities to that of some of the great college players at the time, including Fowler. It had been his dream.

Watching these boys scramble and bump in their determination to get closer to a "star," then switching to bashful timidity once they did, reminded Jeremy how quickly fame and the quest for attention can move higher on the list of importance in a young life. Yes, he'd been just like that. He thanked God for the path his life had *not* taken. He grabbed his gym bag and his digital camera before stepping out on to the pavement and locking the bus.

As Jeremy walked toward the boys still crowding around Shaun, Nick pulled up. He climbed out of his car wearing basketball shorts and a matching T-shirt. He motioned his head toward the mob of boys. "You weren't kidding when you said you would need help with containment."

Jeremy offered his hand in greeting. "You didn't happen to bring a crowbar with you? Otherwise, we may never get them off Shaun and into the rec center to play basketball."

After another glance toward the frenzy of youthful adoration ahead of them, Nick slung his bag over his shoulder. "Were we ever that fan crazy?"

"Don't go trying to sound all mature and above their thrill at meeting someone famous. I heard the awe in your voice last month when you thought Abby was bringing him to one of our games."

"Yeah, well, that was different."

Jeremy shook his head and moved in behind the boys. "Guys," he said, and then with more force, "guys, give Mr. Fowler some breathing room. You have all afternoon to hang out with him and play some ball. He's the one who invited us. Don't give him a reason to send us home early."

His words worked their way through the crowd, and the boys eased back like an ebbing tide, until there was a small opening flanked on both sides by grinning teenage faces. Jeremy was at one end and NBA All-Star Shaun Fowler at the other. He reined in his own fanboy moment and walked up to Shaun.

"Pastor Walker, it's great to finally meet you and some of the youth from your church."

They shook hands. An action Jeremy did countless times in his job. Shaun's grip was firm, as if they were gauging each other's strength.

"A-hem."

Jeremy swiveled his head and grinned. "Oh, sorry. Shaun, may I introduce Nick Delaney. He's on the finance committee at the church, as well. He also works with our youth, and he's Pemberly's newest city councilman."

Shaun's hand came forward. "Nice to meet you."

Nick grinned like one of the teenagers. "It's an honor. Thanks for having us."

With the formalities over, Shaun brought his palms together and slid them against each other while scanning the group of boys. "Let's head inside and get you guys settled. You can meet some of our group before we start working on technique."

A unified "Woo-hoo" came from the boys as Shaun led everyone inside the gymnasium-style building. Jeremy looked around, taking in the high gloss of the court and the bleacher seats, with the digital scoreboards mounted on the front and back walls. They walked single-file along the edge of the court on rubberized matting.

In the far corner, past the bleachers, they went through a set of glass double doors. Along the wall at their left was a huge kitchen. It was separated from an open space the size of the gym they'd just walked through by a half wall supporting a glittering, black, granite countertop.

Boys in sizes comparable to Jeremy's crew were lounging in chairs, some with earbuds linking them to handheld electronics. Others hunched forward, their devices cradled in their hands as their thumbs swirled and dipped, typing out text messages. They all looked up when the doors clicked closed.

"Gather round, guys." Shaun motioned to the boys at the tables.

Both groups traded surreptitious looks as they mingled into a relaxed half circle around Shaun, Nick and him. Jeremy was still taking in the layout of the room and the lighting. There were rows of collapsed round tables leaning against the far wall with chairs stacked in between. This room could easily seat five hundred or more.

The stainless steel doors of the kitchen were propped open. The room was deep. The appliances were spaced far apart with cabinets next to each, providing long, wide surfaces on which to set containers. Just the kitchen alone was large enough to hold both the kitchen and seating area of Grace Community's fellowship hall. Jeremy's mind was taking in all the details, comparing the layout to what the architect had presented for their new kitchen. Here, the island workstations and the two sets of sinks positioned far apart would ensure food prep and cleanup didn't collide.

His first inclination was to call Abby and rattle off the changes he wanted incorporated into their design based on the ideas bouncing around in his head. He stopped himself when his hand went to the phone clipped to his belt. Not his job. At least, not to speak to Abby directly. He would make his suggestions at the next committee meeting.

Nick ambled over and stood beside him. "Plotting and planning how to give the architect more work to do?" He motioned with his head. "How much of this do you want incorporated into the kitchen design Marty's almost finished with?"

Busted. Jeremy tossed him a wry grin. "All of it."

"Greedy, that's what you are. First, you want an air-conditioned place to play basketball. Now you want a kitchen tricked out to all but cook and clean up after itself. I think you're getting lazy in your old age."

Shaun came up between them and clapped them each on the shoulder. "Want a tour?"

Jeremy glanced at him, trying to tone down his excitement. Today was supposed to be about the boys, but Shaun's foundation had built this center. Everything Jeremy had seen so far was exactly what he'd envisioned and prayed for when the idea of a new recreation center for Pemberly became his mission.

God reveals His plans to us when it's time. Today, it was time. "Please. I'd like to grab some shots of the layout of that kitchen to take back to our architect. Our kitchen will be about that size, but we haven't settled on the final design."

Nick excused himself before following the boys back into the gym.

Shaun directed him toward the open kitchen doors. "I thought you'd want to do some reconnaissance while you were here. Abby was telling me the other night about your plans to use the center to reach more of the community. She is one amazing woman."

He stopped and stared straight into Shaun's eyes. "Yes, she is. In more ways than you can imagine."

Shaun slanted his head to the side and studied him

for a moment, then nodded. "I thought that was the way of things."

Jeremy knew what Shaun meant, and worse, he knew it was untrue. He had no claim—no right—where Abby was concerned. Yet he couldn't bring himself to deny the assumption either. His personal feelings for Abby had no place here today. And working with this man who embodied everything he'd dreamed of becoming in his youth was the path God wanted him to walk today.

It was a test involving his heart and soul. Both for his vocation and his future. Even though he was facing both at the same time, he needed to settle the first before he could consider the second. Because without a solid foundation with God, he had no future.

Jeremy rolled his shoulders and prayed the words he needed to say would come. "Abby and I are friends. I cherish our connection. We work together on countless projects within the church." He nudged his head in the direction of the gym where Nick had gone with the boys. "Nick is my best friend. He's marrying Abby's best friend next month. Her life and mine have been intertwined for a long time." He released a chest-tightening breath. "But friends is all we are to each other. I'm not willing to risk what I know we have on the chance of something more. It—she—means too much to me."

"So you wouldn't have a problem with me spending time with her that isn't related to her work for the church and rec center?"

Jeremy's teeth ground together, but he forced the

words through his rigid jaw. "No, I have no claim on Abby's time or her interests."

Shaun glanced at his watch. "Well, I'm glad that's settled." He motioned around the massive room. "I have a set of plans for this room's layout and utility needs. I'll have the center's director send you a copy for your architect." He smiled a bit more broadly. "I'll leave you to take some pictures before you join the kids. The trainers will have assessed their skills by now and grouped them based on what we need to work on the most. Take your time, and let me know if you have any questions." Shaun left him standing in the middle of a kitchen bigger than his house.

Jeremy snapped a few pictures of the room but wasn't far behind. The cheers and groans of energetic boys guided him back to the gym and the basketball court. Shaun had a group of six older boys huddled around him as he pivoted, then jumped, tossing a straight shot into the basket with the *swish* of nothing but net. Three other men had the younger teens grouped around them in separate corners of the court, demonstrating arm rotation and wrist position on release. The youngest group was practicing dribbling and bringing the ball through their legs as they changed direction.

Overall, the scene mirrored a college-sponsored training camp. Nick was sitting on the lowest bleacher behind the older boys with a towel slung around his neck and his hair stuck to his head, damp with sweat.

"Dude, I don't care what those sports announcers said about him being out of the game because of his bum knee. He wiped the floor with me in less than ten minutes." Nick twisted the cap off a Gatorade and took a long swallow.

Jeremy laughed. "Or, you're older than you thought you were. And getting engaged has cut your practice time in half."

"What? Are you saying I'm slacking?"

Jeremy picked up the ball on the floor in front of Nick and set it spinning on his finger. "If the shoe fits…"

A loose ball hit the bleacher next to Jeremy, and he looked up.

Shaun's gaze was trained on him. He put a high arc on the ball for the return throw. Shaun stretched wide and caught it one-handed. He swept the group with a look and nodded toward Nick before settling his gaze back on Jeremy. "I hear you play a pretty good game. Want to try a little one-on-one?" He put the ball to spinning on his finger, slapping it with his other hand, increasing the rotation speed. "It works better if the boys see the moves in action. I wore your friend there out in less than a quarter. Let's see how long you last."

Jeremy caught the ball Shaun chest-passed to him with both hands before it hit his face. His eyes never left Shaun. "Anything for the kids."

"Watch him. He likes to fake with his bad knee, then comes back and takes the shot, pivoting off of it," Nick warned while Jeremy emptied his pockets on to the bench.

"Thanks." He handed Nick the keys to the bus.

He'd known this would happen. Shaun was a com-
petitor. On and off the court. He was interested in
Abby, and Jeremy was a roadblock. And on the court—
Shaun's court—Jeremy was the underdog in too many
ways to count. But David had been, too. And Goliath
still fell because of one little stone.

Right at fifteen minutes of play, with the score tied,
Jeremy faked toward Shaun's bad knee. He tried to
push off that foot and block Jeremy's surge upward toward the basket…and hit the floor because of a slick
spot on the court. Jeremy gripped the rim and hung
in the air for a five count after the *whoosh* of his winning slam dunk.

One of the trainers called time. He caught the towel
Nick tossed him before their boys rushed him on the
court. He high-fived them with one hand and wiped
his face on the towel with the other while walking to
where Shaun was sitting on the floor, his arms draped
over his knees. Nothing could have stopped the grin
spreading on his face as he reached down and offered
the NBA All-Star his hand. "Good game."

"You tore me up. You should have tried out for the
pros."

Except that. The little zing of victory was gone. He
tugged Shaun back to his feet. "We all can't be NBA
superstars."

For Jeremy, the shiny brightness of fun faded to a
duller and duller shade of reality for the rest of the afternoon. The boys' enjoyment of the day and their sense
of accomplishment had them holding their shoulders
straighter with their chests puffed out as they walked

out of the gym. Jeremy shook hands with Shaun and the trainers, thanking them for making the day special for the boys.

Shaun walked with them out to the parking lot and waited. Jeremy cranked the bus and started the AC. The boys climbed aboard without a single complaint. That alone wasn't normal, but appreciated. They'd played so hard they were too tired for their usual picking and poking at each other. Jeremy left the doors open and came around to stand with Shaun and Nick in front of Nick's car.

"It was great meeting you." Jeremy nodded toward the bus full of boys relaxed in their seats. "And thank you for helping us bring opportunities like today to a lot more kids."

Shaun accepted his outstretched hand. "I enjoyed it. I like giving kids an opportunity to push themselves athletically—to discover just how much they're capable of if given the chance. Your kids are good kids. You're doing a great work through them."

"Thanks. It's a group effort between the church staff, our volunteers and the kids' parents. Some come from homes that don't encourage hope in being anything more than what their parents are. As a church, we're trying to help them see that God looks at what's on the inside, so they understand their choices aren't just seen on the outside."

"That's a good goal." He held his hands up and took a step back. "I'm not that big on church. But, hey, we each go at helping others the way that works best for us."

His comment pricked Jeremy's conscience. Even

though he knew his relationship with Abby was strained right now, she was his friend, and he owed it to her to look out for her. "Abby's character is a reflection of the depth of her faith. If you're around her very much, it won't take long for you to see her goodness goes soul-deep."

Nick quirked an eyebrow at Jeremy. He looked back at Shaun, holding his gaze, willing him to understand that Abby was nothing like the women he usually dated. She was beyond compare. And he had better respect her. Or else.

"Abby. Abby." Katherine laid her hand on her arm.

Abby jumped. "Sorry. My mind was somewhere else."

"Mmm-hmm. And who was it there with?"

The conversation was cut short when the hostess at Del Sol approached. They followed her to a quiet booth in the corner and accepted their menus. Abby straightened her silverware next to her plate, her finger running across the handle of her butter knife. Where was the bread? She was starving. Trying not to plot someone's murder did that to her.

Their waiter arrived with a stainless steel pitcher of ice water and a basket of bread still warm from the oven. Abby placed her order for grilled chicken and steamed vegetables while Katherine stuck with her usual salad.

"Worried you won't fit into your dress if you eat something besides lettuce?"

"Ha-ha. For your information, I'm so busy I forget to eat lunch half the time. I've lost five pounds. Merisel is going to have a fit if she has to tuck the waist in again."

Abby leaned forward. "There are worse things in the world than needing the waist taken in on your wedding dress. That's what you get for choosing that gorgeous, fitted bodice gown with enough tulle to outfit a sailboat. But you look stunning in it, so I guess it's worth it."

Katherine studied her, dragging the moment of silence out for a few heartbeats. "I have wedding jitters as an excuse for not eating. You don't."

Abby stopped mangling the piece of bread she'd been craving before it arrived but now was turning into a mound of soft crumbs. "I'm fine."

"No, you're not. Nick said Jeremy and Shaun got along well when they took the boys to meet him. The outer walls are going up on the recreation center. I'm not calling you in the middle of the night, claiming I made a mistake when I said I'd marry Nick. Gina is singing your praises at the office, until I'm tempted to give her to you full-time, since she's happier working with you, and I feel like I'm holding her back from reaching her employment potential."

"Wow. That was more information, both personal and professional, than you've ever shared with me in a day, let alone an hour."

"Nice redirect, but I went to law school, too. I can spot an evasive answer from further away than across the table. Spill." Katherine moved the basket of bread out of reach.

Abby's shoulders drooped. "Jeremy and Shaun's meeting did go well. Too well, in fact."

"How so?"

"Jeremy claims the kitchen at the center they visited is exactly what he envisioned for ours. Shaun sent him a set of plans so we could have the architect do an assessment and see what the bank's position would be on altering the original submission."

"Will it be a problem?"

"No. The projected cost for the new design is actually a little less, so the bank is all for it. Shaun called me yesterday and asked me out."

"Wait." Katherine scooted back in her seat, drawing herself up straight. "You've been meeting with Shaun for over two months and taking Gina with you. She's so obnoxious the next day, with her 'Shaun said,' 'Shaun prefers,' it's almost nauseating except for how it makes Toby scowl. That, I enjoy."

Abby frowned at her.

"Right. Now, I'm wandering off the designated path. So, I'm taking it that this outing doesn't include Gina and might have more of a couples theme to it."

"The Atlanta YMCA is honoring him and his foundation's work with kids from low-income families. He asked me to go as his date."

Katherine held her water goblet in her hand, swirling the liquid, causing the ice cubes to plink against the sides. "There's nothing wrong with you going out with him if you like him and you're attracted to him. Are you attracted to him?"

"He's nice."

"Hmm. So he doesn't make your heart go pitty-patter?"

"That doesn't have to happen for me to go on a date. I know I'm overthinking his invitation, but I can't help wondering how it could affect my working relationship with him on the project. Or, what Jeremy will think."

Katherine cut her off, waving her butter knife in the air. "Jeremy has no say in your personal life."

"But—"

"After the way he's acted toward you, no. He doesn't deserve your consideration."

The desire to argue faded, leaving her eyes stinging with unwanted and unshed tears. Katherine reached over and squeezed her hand, holding it tight. When Abby met her concerned gaze, there was no judgment, no pity. For that, she would be forever grateful. She drew in a fortifying breath through her nose and eased it out through her mouth in an effort to calm her confused thoughts.

"I know you care for him. I'm glad he has someone like who does. But that doesn't mean he deserves your care or your kindness. I don't know what internal battle he's fighting, but until he's willing to share the truth with you, all you can do—all any of us can do—is pray for him."

"I know. When Shaun asked me to the dinner, it was flattering to know he was asking me to go for myself and not because of the center." Abby smiled her thanks. "I think I'll call him and accept his invitation when I get back to the office."

Their waiter stopped at their table and presented a small serving tray with two pieces of the richest, most decadent chocolate cake Abby had ever seen. Katherine whimpered. Abby grinned.

"Compliments of a secret admirer."

Katherine's head whipped around, taking in the other patrons. "Who?"

"Uh-uh-uh." The waiter wagged a finger at her. "A *secret* admirer." He set a small gold-rimmed plate in front of each of them.

"I guess you won't need an extra appointment with Madame Merisel after all."

Katherine forked a small bite into her mouth and sighed. Or maybe it was a moan. "No, I won't. And if you don't eat all of yours, I'm claiming that, too."

Abby laughed. "Your curiosity is easily quashed with chocolate."

"Well, I'm guessing this is from Nick. Today is the five-month anniversary of when he proposed."

"Ahhh." Abby nodded. "Only one more month until you're Mrs. Nicholas Delaney. Sometimes it's still hard to imagine Nick as the glob of mush he turns into when you're around. But it's very sweet." Her eyes watered, but not for herself this time. It was for the happiness lighting her friend's huge grin.

Then Katherine leaned forward with the most earnest expression on her face. "It will happen for you, too. It might not be with Jeremy, but I'm praying that God sends you the best man on earth. One who will love you with everything he has, just like you deserve."

Abby tried to keep smiling, but her heart froze at Katherine's words. *It might not be with Jeremy.*

She didn't want that with someone else.

Chapter 6

Abby paused outside Jeremy's office door, staring at his name etched on the bronze nameplate. The dread weighing her down at the thought of the coming conversation only made her third-guess her decision to accept Shaun's dinner invitation. After a stern internal lecture over how ridiculous she was being, she rapped her knuckles against the solid wood.

Jeremy opened the door immediately. It caught her off guard. "Hi."

He stepped back, motioning her inside. "Hey. What brings you by today?"

She shot him a smile, flashing more teeth than usual. She shouldn't be this nervous. Honestly. He was her friend. She wasn't accountable to him for whom she dated. They were doing better since he'd come back from spending the day with Shaun and the youths. He acted excited again about the center and how many more kids and parents they could reach for Jesus once it was built. The foundation had been poured and things were moving right along.

Here goes nothing. "I, um, I wanted to let you know things are going well. I know you can see the construction progress out your office window. The bank approved all the changes to the kitchen area. Marty has given the general contractor the new plans, and he's changing the materials order now, so it will be as if that was the original design when they start on the interior."

"That's great. And, yeah, it's hard to ignore the construction with the cement trucks and all the hammering."

She glanced toward his picture window in a panic. "Oh, no. It isn't affecting services, is it?"

He shook his head. "No, everyone's excited that construction is underway."

"Good. That's great."

He moved back to one of the chairs facing his desk and waited until she sat down before going around and taking his own seat. "Why do I feel like you aren't here to update me on the progress of the construction?"

Her head shot up, and her gaze tangled with his. "Well. Um. That is—because that isn't what I wanted to talk to you about."

He eased back in his chair, watching her, searching her face. "Did something happen with Shaun?"

"No! I mean, not anything bad." She let out a huff of

breath, tired of the walk down Eggshell Lane. "Shaun asked me out to dinner."

"You and Gina have been going to dinner with him for a while now. Why are you telling me about this meeting?" His eyes widened. "Oh. That kind of dinner."

"The YMCA is honoring him and the Kids for Sports foundation next week. He asked me to go as his date." Then for no reason she could understand, she kept talking, telling him way more than he needed to know. "He said the press only shows him with women whose appeal is limited to their looks."

He was quiet for a few moments, and she resisted squirming in her chair, looking at anything but him. "He said it would be nice to have dinner with someone interested in more than who was on the cover of the latest fashion magazine."

"Yes, he was singing your praises when we met."

"He did? You discussed me with him?"

"He thought maybe you and I were more than friends. But, don't worry. I let him know I have no claim on you and that you were available."

Someone could have thrown her in a swimming pool full of ice water, and she wouldn't have shivered any more than she did at his words. How dare he speak for her? "You told him I was available. You don't have the right—"

"That's what I said. He was just making sure he wasn't poaching—"

"Poaching!" She was on her feet, her nails biting into her palms to keep herself from reaching across his desk and snatching him up by his hair. She walked in a circle, fighting against the anger whipping her emotions into the churning force of a Cat Four hurricane. She swung back to face him, her fists planted on her hips. "Who do you think you are? I'm a thirty-year-old woman living in a democratic society with the right to vote. I'm an attorney-at-law and my father is a US senator. I've stood on platforms when my mother couldn't, before thousands of people, holding a Bible as my father took his oath of office. I decide who I date and who I don't. You, of all people, have no authority to discuss my dating status with anyone."

Something she said must have penetrated his ministerial control because he was up and coming around his desk. Good. She was going to wring his pious neck.

He stopped mere inches before colliding with her and peered down his nose at her. "Yes, you thrive in the spotlight. And *I* know better than you, exactly how much of a right I don't have to say anything about who you date." His voice was deep, gravelly. His breath hot as his words pushed out between his clenched teeth.

"You're the press's favorite feature. Everyone loves to photograph you. You smile so carefree, as if you were born in the spotlight. And every time I see your picture in the paper, the truth of how separate our lives and our goals are slaps me in the face."

"The spotlight? I had no choice. My father's career as a public servant required his family be onboard whether we wanted to or not."

He flung his hand in the air as if tossing her reply

away. "Oh, please. You bask in the attention. You aren't a diva about it. But no matter what you're doing, you always have time to stop and pose when there's a photo op. I admire the fact that you use your celebrity for good. You're a wonderful person. A true Christian woman. Shaun is lucky you're interested in him."

His last words should have cooled her anger, but she was human. And right now, the urge to err was winning by a mile. "Your fear of having your picture taken doesn't justify this warped view you have of what it's like to live my life." Her throat was raw with the burn of fury, her words slashing at him like daggers, meant to wound him as he was wounding her.

"You think I walk into a room, scan it for cameras and then avoid them because I want to? Don't you think I'd change that if I could?" His voice grew louder with each word.

"I don't know!" she yelled back. "All I know is when it came time to step up and do something that would introduce more kids to Christ, you ran scared. I've made excuses for your fear, but if you had the faith you challenge us to have on Sunday mornings, you could have done what was *your* responsibility, not mine."

"You think I'm a coward? You have no idea the sacrifices I've made for my family. I could have been Shaun Fowler. I would have made millions, and I would have made a difference. But my father almost died, and my life changed overnight. No one asked me what I wanted. No one cared that I could have been a star. I just had to shut it all away and do this." He was in her face. His voice was guttural, his chest heaving. He squeezed his eyes closed.

"Are you saying you never wanted to be a minister? Then you're living a lie. You've been misleading all of us."

The panicked terror on his face tempered some of the anger surging through her veins.

"That isn't what I meant." He stepped away, putting his desk between them. "After my family moved here and I met Katherine, God helped me see my life differently. He showed me how I could make a difference in people's eternal lives. That is more important than anything I could do with all the money in the world. I'm thankful God brought me here. I love almost everything about my life. Hiding from cameras and the constant fear that my face might appear in the paper or some other form of media subconsciously guides every choice I make. It's why I haven't married."

Her heart stopped. "You wanted to marry someone?"

The anguish on his face as he met her gaze called to the twisting ache in her stomach.

"I can't marry. I can't even date as long as this fear has control of my life."

"You're the one letting it control your life. You know God will give you the strength to overcome it if you ask Him."

The heat of anger flared in his eyes again. "No, Abby. It isn't that simple. I pray every day for God to deliver me from the prison of this fear. He hasn't. And, it's time I faced the truth. He won't."

"What? How can you give up? This is your life. You, more than anyone, should have the faith to know there is always a solution to a problem—through God."

His laugh was haunting, heckling, even. "You and your perfect life wouldn't understand."

All pity and misplaced sympathy died. "My mother was diagnosed with demophobia two months after my father ran for his first office."

"Abby, I don't—"

"It's the fear of crowds. When I was growing up, I never questioned why we didn't join the mobs at the mall on Black Friday the way all my friends did. I've never liked being pushed and pulled by strangers, so I didn't think it was odd."

The words were tumbling past her lips faster than her brain could screen them. She let them run free. "I was thirteen. Daddy was giving a speech, and my mother was waiting with me offstage. We were supposed to join him on the dais when he finished. A group of twenty or so reporters had come in through the back entrance, pushing up against us. My mom turned around and couldn't see through the throng. She crumpled to the floor in a ball, sobbing."

As she talked, Jeremy took her elbow and steered her to one of a set of cushioned chairs beside a coffee table. "Seeing her like that, I've never been so frightened in my life. I screamed. The reporters stepped back, but they kept snapping pictures. The flashes blinded me. I had a brown belt in tae kwon do. I put myself between my mother and the reporters and took up a defensive stance. One guy stepped close, and I did a crescent kick that knocked his camera out of his hand. He lunged at me."

Jeremy inhaled sharply, reaching to take her hand.

The left side of her mouth lifted in a half smile. "By then my father had arrived. Needless to say, my dad bought the reporter a new camera and I think a gold tooth."

She hadn't planned to say any of this when she arrived. Today's visit was to tell him she was going on a real date with Shaun. Because somewhere in her foolish, fairy tale–believing heart, she'd hoped he cared enough about her to ask her not to say yes. But he hadn't, and now all she wanted to do was leave. To have her daddy hold her the way he had that day after the reporters left, and tell her how strong she was.

She didn't feel very strong right now. She had bared her heart to this man, served it up on a platter, and he'd said, "No, thanks, I'm good." She was done waiting. She had a life of purpose to live. And it didn't include Jeremy Walker and the fear he was willing to embrace rather than fight. Her mother still waited backstage at each of her dad's speeches. But two security men made sure no one crowded her. And Abby didn't practice tae kwon do anymore.

"Wow. Remind me not to push you."

He was making light of their conversation. Of course he was. They were just friends. And most of that relationship came from forced contact through Nick, Kat and the church. She stood to leave. "Well, I said what I came to say. I need to go shopping for a new dress."

Yes, she was that petty. It made her feel better for about a second and a half. But he would never see her cry. Not ever.

Jeremy sat, rolling his minibasketball between his hands staring at the chair where Abby had sat an hour ago. Where she'd been when she told him about a very private, personal moment during her and her mother's lives. It was one more thing to admire her for—her bravery. Her willingness to take on whatever battle came her way. And he'd acted like a spoiled brat, snarling at her because she was living her full life without him.

"Well, you're a sorry sight to see." Nick stood in the doorway with his hands in his pockets, jingling his change, shaking his head.

"I've seen you look about the same once or twice."

Nick came in and took Abby's earlier spot. "Yep. So, are you this glum because of a woman, too?"

"Not today, Nick. I'm not in a joking mood."

"No, you're in a whiny, pity-party mood. Besides, Kat sent me."

Jeremy rolled his eyes. "Let me guess, Abby's already called and told her what a jerk I was today. And you just happened to be in the area and decided to stop by with an attitude adjustment." He squeezed the ball tighter. "Well, here's a news flash. I don't need anyone telling me what I should and shouldn't do. I already have a rule book. There are things about me I can't tell anyone. Why doesn't matter. It's just a fact. And the sooner Abby realizes that, the happier she'll be. I'm not a superstar like Shaun Fowler. I can't make her dreams come true. I can't give her the world."

"I came by—"

The minibasketball Jeremy had been squeezing shot across the room and banked off the bookshelf, rolling to a stop at Nick's feet.

He bent and picked the ball up, tossing it up and catching it. "So, you know they're going out."

Jeremy sank lower into his chair. "Yeah. He's taking her to a fancy dinner in Atlanta where they're honoring him for all his philanthropic greatness. They'll be the most photogenic couple there. If she marries him, even their kids will be gorgeous."

Nick threw the ball like a baseball and nailed him right between the eyes.

Jeremy scrambled to his feet, shaking off the shock of the hit. "Hey. What do you think you're doing?"

"I don't know. You're the one acting stupid. I thought I'd join the party." Nick got up and moved around him, blocking the path to his desk.

"It isn't stupid."

"Then what is it?"

Jeremy ground his teeth together and tried nudging him clear with his shoulder. "I can't tell you any more than I could tell Abby. So, lay off me."

Nick put his palm flat against Jeremy's chest, holding him in place. "Wait. I'm your friend. I'm worried about you."

"And I said I'm fine."

"No, you're not. You're the most easygoing, happy guy I know. It's part of your charm. But lately, you've been edgy, combative, angry and downright surly on a couple of occasions. Take my concern in the guise of friendship, or as a church member, or your basketball teammate, or even your attorney. Whichever one sparks your brain to start looking for a solution."

"I don't have an attorney."

"Maybe you need one." Nick stepped back and sat down in front of his desk, propping his feet on the edge. "We're the most expensive therapists around, but if it can be cathartic for you, I'll listen for free. Or have you done anything illegal, aside from really ticking my fiancée off with your unkind treatment of her best friend?"

This wasn't happening to him. He didn't have it within him to argue right now. "Really? You put your shoes on your minister's desk. That's some kind of respect. This is God's house and His furniture. I'd move my feet if I were you before He sends a bolt of lightning through the window."

Nick dropped his feet and chuckled. "That sounds more like my basketball buddy. I knew he was in there somewhere."

"I never left. I'm fine. Abby's still mad because I wouldn't do those interviews. Then, when I cautioned her about Shaun, she was offended by my concern. Her life is going in one direction, and mine is headed in another."

"Yeah, about that. Can you buy a new compass or recalibrate your GPS?"

"I and my issues with photo ops have no place in Abby's extrafriendly media life. It just took this project to show us how different we are."

"Do I need to ask someone else to perform the ceremony?"

The words hit Jeremy in the stomach, forcing the air out of his lungs. "You don't want me to marry you and Kat?"

Nick glanced up and froze. "No. No, that is not what I'm saying. We're good. You're good. Kat doesn't want anyone else doing the ceremony. But she is worried about Abby."

Jeremy closed and opened his eyes on an extended blink. "Abby left here not an hour ago after telling me she's dating Shaun. She's fine. Her life is picture-perfect." The realization of how true that was had the burning in his chest spreading to his stomach. "Can we talk about something besides her, like what you want to do for your bachelor party?"

"*I* have to tell you what to do? I thought the best man planned the party."

"Your father is your best man. I'm happy to let him organize the festivities."

"Oh, no, you don't." Nick pointed his finger at him. "His idea of fun involves a speechwriter and an election strategist."

Jeremy chuckled, his amusement real and welcome. "So, you think a bachelor party arranged by your minister would be more fun? We'll all be safe from the cameras. There won't be anything happening exciting enough you'll want pictures."

"Whatever you plan has to be more enjoyable than the political fund-raiser my dad would orchestrate."

"Are we talking a sports theme? An outdoor theme? A movie binge? What? I can make it happen."

"Kat said Abby and Gina are treating her to a day at the spa."

Jeremy enunciated his words clearly, so there would be no confusion. "I will not plan nor pay for anything that involves you getting your nails buffed."

"Not what I meant. I was more intrigued with the idea of doing something relaxing that included a few guys instead of a big party."

He nodded. "Got it. Stuart's father owns a charter fishing boat. We could drive over to the coast on a Friday afternoon and be out on the open water early the next morning."

Nick drummed his fingers on the desk a few times while he mulled over the suggestion. "Okay. I was thinking of renting a suite at Turner Field and catching a Braves game, but I haven't been fishing since I was a kid. This could be fun."

"Am I inviting your father and Judge Pierce?"

"It might be best. The judge can throw Dad overboard if he starts talking about me running for state representative before I've finished my first year as a city council member."

Jeremy paused, more for himself than Nick, before mentioning the next name. "What about Toby Hendricks?"

"What about him?"

Jeremy threw him a stern look, complete with raised eyebrow.

"Oh, right. Is Gina being nice to him again?"

"He scored some major brownie points with her when he rescued her while she was stranded on the interstate with a flat tire—during a tornado warning."

Nick's jaw dropped open. "You're kidding, right?"

Jeremy shook his head. "Nope, he even talked his editor into letting him do a feature on the highway patrol since they helped him find her exact location. I don't know how he does it, but somehow he manages to always land on his feet. He's been at every celebration we've had so far. But if he tries snapping any pictures on this trip, it's possible he and his camera might end up swimming back to shore."

Nick got to his feet and began a slow amble around the room. "I wish you'd explain this avoidance of cameras to me."

"Sorry, Abby would be the first to hear my explanation if I had one."

"Then, why did you tell Shaun she was fair game?"

"Because Shaun's a better match for her than I'll ever be, camera phobia or not."

"Are you moonlighting as a church singles matching service now? Pastor Pairing or something like that?"

"Nick, I'm really tired of talking about Abby and Shaun and dating. Can we move on to something else?"

"I'll say this, then I'm done. Okay?" He walked back over to him.

Jeremy's spine stiffened, and he braced himself for the worst, but he stared Nick in the eyes. "Go ahead."

"Send the woman flowers. You don't have to do an entire building full of bouquets the way I did. But send her a pretty arrangement with a note saying you're sorry."

"I—"

"You are sorry about upsetting her, aren't you?"

"Yes, but I can't do anything to change the circumstances. So, how will flowers make it better?"

"They won't. But the gesture will show her she matters to you. Whether the two of you should or will be together is in God's hands. But I don't believe you're in each other's lives for nothing. Don't you miss her?"

That wasn't a question at all, more of a given.

"Yeah, I do." *Every time I breathe.*

"I think she misses you, too." Nick dropped his hand on Jeremy's shoulder and squeezed. "Send the flowers."

Jeremy let out a long breath. "I will."

"That's my line." After a snappy salute, he left.

Now that he was alone, the solitude of his office didn't offer the peace it usually did. He pulled his keys from his desk drawer and left, taking the path past the construction area on his way to his car. They had poured the foundation. The concrete blocks that would make up the outside walls were being cemented into place, starting at the corners.

The area around his heart ached. His joy at watching this new outreach for Christ take shape battled with the insurmountable vastness of the divide separating him from Abby. The tug on his soul to open up to God was strong. For the past few days, he'd spent his prayer time preparing his sermons and focusing on the needs of the congregation, as he should.

But he needed to spend some time on his knees,

seeking God's guidance and comfort, for himself. His whole being would benefit and his hope would be renewed. He drove home humming a favorite song—"Give Me Jesus."

Chapter 7

Abby stood in front of the fridge with the door propped against her hip. The pale white glow of the low-wattage bulb reflected off the stainless-steel finish of the surrounding appliances. The contents on the shelf were as unappetizing to her as her own company was.

Her father draped his arm around her and drew her in, dropping a kiss on the top of her head. "What are you doing up at this hour?"

She stepped back and let the door swing closed. He switched on the light over the breakfast nook before coming over to lean against the island behind her with his arms crossed loosely over his chest.

After a deep sigh, she offered him a weak attempt at a smile. "I didn't eat much tonight at dinner, and I thought I was hungry."

"Hungry or sad?"

Her smile was real this time. "Confused."

He opened the cabinet and pulled out two large mugs. She got the milk from the refrigerator. He took the jug from her and poured some into each mug before putting one into the microwave. In the pantry, she found the box of hot chocolate. She laid it on the counter.

After he switched mugs in the microwave, she dumped one of the packets into the steaming milk and stirred it with a spoon. After she'd done the same for the other one, they brought their drinks to the table.

"You didn't enjoy your dinner with that basketball star?" Her father blew on the liquid to cool it.

"It was fine. He introduced me to a lot of people who would really like to meet you." She tried for one of Gina's impish grins.

"Me? You were on a date with a celebrity, and the people around him were trying to network with you to reach me?"

"You're a very important man. One of the movers and shakers."

"I'm too old to shake anything."

"Daddy. That isn't what I meant."

He grinned and reached out to chuck her under the chin with a curved finger. "I know. So, why were you out with this fella when I thought you had an eye on our pastor?"

Abby rotated her mug between her hands, drawing on its warmth. "Shaun's foundation is funding the majority of the building costs for our new recreation center. Gina and I have spent many a dinner with him going over financials and the promotion of the project."

Her father laid his hand over hers. "That isn't what I asked you."

"The finance committee's plan to raise the necessary funds to begin construction involved Jeremy doing some interviews and minor speaking engagements. He refused."

"Refused? Why?"

"That's what I keep asking him, and he keeps saying he can't tell me."

He pushed their mugs out of the way, then took both of her hands. "You've argued with him, haven't you?"

She wouldn't meet his eyes. He liked Jeremy both as a minister and as a man. But since Jeremy was their minister, her father wouldn't be happy knowing she'd unloaded her temper on him. "I was provoked each time."

"Did you go out with Shaun to get back at Jeremy?"

"Of course not." How could he assume *she* was the problem?

"Then why your sudden disinterest in Jeremy?"

"Daddy, I'm not the one throwing up roadblocks. Jeremy and I are friends. Or I thought we were. You weren't there when he saw the list of interviews I'd scheduled. It was as if he became someone else. I've asked him several times to help me understand why he can't be interviewed, so I could work on a new plan that was more comfortable for him. He shut me down, flat. He wouldn't talk about it. Wouldn't even give me a hint as to what his specific objection was to the proposal. No interviews and no cameras. That's why I found Shaun. He does interviews and smiles pretty for the camera when prompted."

He watched her, his brow creased. "Jeremy can't be afraid of public speaking. He's perfectly at ease in the pulpit. There was a request for the morning services to be broadcast live over the internet a few years back. He asked that we stream the audio and offered a compelling argument for not using a video feed. Hmm. That's interesting." He handed her back her mug. "Drink up before it cools."

"Is Mom any better?"

"Some. The new cough medicine is working. She can sleep for several hours now before it wakes her up again. This cold has really made her tired. She isn't going to Washington with me next week. I'll be back before the weekend. Maybe by then she'll be caught up on her rest. But you still haven't said what's really bothering you. We've talked about Jeremy's lack of cooperation and Shaun's fancy dinner. What haven't you told me?"

Abby blew out a breath that ruffled her bangs. "I've always been attracted to Jeremy. You know that. And, I had hoped that someday he and I…"

He rose and came around to her side of the table, nudging her farther over on the bench. "I know, baby girl. Are your feelings hurt? Is it something he can say he's sorry for and you'll be able to forgive him?"

Her head moved side to side, and she closed her eyes against the sting of tears. She didn't want to cry. She hated crying. It made her head hurt and her nose stuffy. And it wouldn't do a thing to fix the problem. She blew out another breath, trying to calm her emotions and stop the flow of tears. But she was like a leaky faucet, still dripping away. "Every time I see him, our conversations circle back to his lack of support for the recreation center. And every time, he says he's sorry. And then we go right back to me needing to know what I can expect of him as far as support and him shutting me out."

"Maybe it is something he can't tell you."

"Daddy, he was in my office, and I told him whatever he said wouldn't leave the room. He knows I'm an attorney. He knows attorney-client privilege is as binding as patient confidentiality. Or confessions to a priest. Nothing gets through to him. But I keep hoping, because I can't believe the man I know, the man I care for, can be that cold and unfeeling. He just can't be."

"I know, honey. But you aren't crying because he won't explain his aversion to cameras to you. What is it?"

Abby angled herself on the bench until she faced him. "After Shaun asked me to the dinner, I went to see Jeremy. I told him about the date. He said he'd assured Shaun he wouldn't be poaching on his territory." Her face crumpled, and she grabbed a napkin to blot her eyes. "He handed me over like I was a turkey or a deer. Or worse, a wild boar."

Her dad wrapped her in his arms, pulling her tight against his chest, and let her cry until there were no more tears. He'd always been so strong and solid, protecting her from whatever came at her. Helping her find a solution to her problems. But there was no fixing this. At least not with earthly hands. She trusted God completely, knew He could do anything. So, why did she feel so sad and lost?

Her father used another napkin to wipe the last of her tears away and then pressed his cheek against the top of her head. "Dear Lord, we come to You this night with heavy hearts. But we know that You are the lifter of our spirits, the joy that comes in the morning. I ask, dear Father, that You give my little girl peace in her heart and assurance that You are in control. You see her tears and You know the desires of her heart. And, Lord, we ask that You will give those to her if she will trust You. Help her be strong and ready to act when it's time. And, Lord, You know Jeremy's heart and the battles he's fighting. Strengthen him, guide him and help us to be there for him to show him our love and concern for his heart as he has shown for ours all these years. And if it's within Your plan for him to be with Abby, give them Your wisdom in how to come together for a life that is strong and full of Your love and joy. But if that isn't Your plan for them, give them peace and show them the way You would have them go instead. We love you, Lord, and thank You for Your love for us."

Warmth settled deep within Abby's heart, and she knew it came from her dad's words and the answer of her Heavenly Father. "Thank you, Daddy. I love you."

He hugged her tight, then slid out from the table. She followed, taking both their mugs to the sink, emptying them and then rinsing them.

He waited until she was finished, then caught her

arm, turning her toward him. "You go to bed and get some sleep. This will all work out. It might take a while, but when God has something big planned for us, it doesn't come about in a day." He kissed her cheek before heading toward the back stairs.

Jeremy sat in his office Friday morning, staring at his computer screen. He was supposed to be reviewing the bulletin for Sunday morning's service before it was printed that afternoon. The pages could have been blank for all he absorbed of the lines of words. He hadn't seen Abby since their fight last week. Maybe her dinner with Shaun had gone well. His stomach clenched and his heart pounded, beating against the restrictions on his life that kept him from going after his heart's desire. Abby.

A heavy knock sounded at his door, pulling him from his hopeless musings. He opened the door and came face-to-face with the intimidating frown of Senator Harold Blackmon.

"Senator, sir. What a surprise. Is everything okay?" Jeremy offered a tight smile.

"You tell me." He stepped past him and walked into the room. Leashed tension crackled in the air around him.

"Without saying anything that might cause you to be more upset with me, I assume you aren't here in regard to my preaching or the church." Jeremy closed the door before going back to his desk and taking his seat. He motioned the senator to a chair.

At first, the senator didn't move, just looked at him,

as if he was an organism he was studying under a microscope. He hadn't thought of himself on a molecular level since biology class. He squirmed under the man's heavy perusal, unsure his backbone wouldn't bend in the face of his anger.

"I'm not here as your representative for the federal government. I'm here as a father. Abby's father."

Jeremy pushed back in his chair, dread clawing from his stomach up to the back of his throat. He swallowed hard, forcing it down. "I admit our relationship has been strained lately, but we'll get through it."

"Will you? You made my little girl cry. You can't appreciate what that does to a father. With all my influence and Christian faith, I can't make her feel better." He leaned across the desk until he was in Jeremy's space. "But you can."

"Sir, I understand the frustration you're feeling. I'd do anything, give anything, to keep from hurting Abby. But I can't. It's not that simple." *Lord, please help me know what to say.*

"Sure it is. In fact, your phone should be ringing shortly with what I've prayed and asked God to let become the beginning of a solution. Or at the least, the removal of a huge stumbling block." The senator straightened, then walked over to the section of bookshelves that held different versions of the Bible and selected one.

Jeremy forced himself to finish reviewing the bulletin before any other visitors appeared unannounced. When the phone rang a few minutes later, he glanced across the room at the senator and his relaxed position in the same chair where Abby had sat last week.

It was Dekker. "Is Blackmon there?" His voice was more clipped than usual.

"Yes, the senator's here."

"I'll be there in half an hour."

"Dekker, what's—"

"My boss got a call which encouraged him to call me. Apparently, I'm late for my appointment with you and the senator in your office."

"But—"

"We'll finish this conversation when I get there."

Click. Dekker was gone. Jeremy looked over at the senator again. He was carefully thumbing through the pages. A quickening ran through Jeremy. He'd prayed about a center that the church could use to reach more of the city's youth, believing that as Grace Community's pastor, he would be the one to lead the project. But that wasn't God's plan. In fact, the block walls were going up outside his office window without his doing anything. Abby had been God's emissary for that purpose. Even after the building was completed and the kids were there, he'd be one of many participating in the programs created to show the kids and their parents about God and His love.

He'd still have his weekly basketball games with the older teen boys. But aside from serving as senior pastor, the other ministers, like Stuart, would be the ones leading the big outreach programs at the rec center.

The truth spoke to his heart. Had he taken over God's plan, believing he was the one in charge? The one making this ministry happen? How foolish, how selfish, how human of him. Pride was a constant enemy, distracting him from the truth that God was always in control. If he would forget about grand success happening under *his* leadership and let the True Leader lead, everything would be perfect, just like God's will.

He walked the bulletin out to Mrs. Hall and went over the changes he'd notated. With a few more minutes until Dekker's threat of arrival, he walked down to the conference room and put a pot of coffee on to brew.

Back in his office, the senator was still reading. The thrum of construction drew his gaze, and he pointed his chair toward the window. Two men were busy assembling the bottom section of scaffolding in front of the waist-high outer wall. They were getting taller.

Two quick taps on the door and it came open. Dekker stood there. His eyes scanned the room before landing on Jeremy. "Pastor."

Senator Blackmon laid the Bible on the low table before him and rose to his feet. Jeremy also stood, moving toward Dekker and offering his hand.

"Marshal Dekker, I don't believe you know Senator Blackmon."

Dekker looked past Jeremy to the senator and offered a stiff nod. "Sir."

"Marshal Dekker." The senator's voice was low and stern. His gaze hard.

Jeremy cleared his throat. "Gentlemen, why don't we get comfortable, so we can proceed?" He motioned them back to the small sitting area. Two chairs and a settee flanked the low table holding the Bible the senator had been reading.

Dekker claimed the chair across from the senator's, leaving Jeremy the settee. That little excuse for furniture sat so low, his knees nearly rubbed his chin when he had to sit there. Katherine and Abby had talked him into adding it to the seating arrangement, claiming it was more welcoming to the women when he did premarriage and marital counseling.

In a hope of finding a man-size seat, he walked back to the door and checked the reception desk. Empty. He was tempted to move one of the chairs in front of his desk over to where Dekker and the senator were engaging in a menacing stare competition.

Before joining them, he asked, "Would either of you care for a cup of coffee?"

Both men mumbled a negative. Okay, then. He asked God to lead not just him but the others in the room, so that no one did anything that would be unpleasing to Him. Then he strode over to the little sofa and made himself as comfortable as he could on such an uncomfortable piece of furniture. He sat in tense silence near two men he never dreamed he would see in the same room. Especially if that room was his office.

Senator Blackmon started the conversation. "Jeremy, I want you to tell me what was wrong with the first proposal the committee submitted to you with their plans for how to finance the construction of the new recreation center."

Of course, he would be the one answering the questions. He glanced toward Dekker and quirked his brow, looking for some signal to let him know if the "rules" applied in this setting. And Dekker wasn't giving anything away. No nod. No shake. Nothing. Great. *Lord, please give me Your wisdom.*

"As Abby presented it, they wanted me to do interviews on the local TV news station, the *Sentinel* and some radio stations." He cleared his throat. "I can't have my photograph in the news."

The senator leaned forward, resting his lower arms on his knees, his fingertips grazing each other as they dangled there between his knees. "Is this problem with the media due to a medical condition?"

"Sir?"

"Do you have a phobia of crowds, camera flashes or the media in general, or of having your picture taken?"

"No, sir. I just can't have my picture showing up in the papers."

"And why is that?" This time the senator wasn't looking at him when he asked the question. His eyes were trained on Dekker.

Dekker was leaning back in a negligent slouch, but his knuckles were white where they gripped the arms of the chair. He returned the senator's intense gaze with an icy one, still holding silent.

Something snapped inside Jeremy. On his right sat the law of the land, used to instill order and civility, but through inflexible rules that offered no compassion or understanding for the people those rules were designed to protect.

To his left was a man with the power to influence those rules. To have them changed if they were flawed. A man who applied not only the law of the land, but also the law of a higher principality. One that ruled with love and compassion for its people. He wanted to tell the truth—the whole truth. And he was going to, whether Dekker liked it or not.

"The reason I can't have my picture in the paper or any other media outlet is because my parents and I are in witness protection. That's the first rule we were given when Marshal Dekker and his team relocated us here to Pemberly." He didn't glance at Dekker. He wanted to see the senator's reaction to his answer.

He nodded. "So, that picture of Abby dancing with you, even though it didn't really show your face, was a problem."

Dekker sat up straight. "Senator, your political position has made you a very high-profile figure for the media, especially here. Miss Blackmon, through her active participation in your campaigns and her personal civic projects, draws a lot of media attention. Not only for herself but also for the people around her. That's too big a risk to Jeremy's family for the program."

"My understanding was that the Walkers entered the program voluntarily."

"Everyone enters voluntarily. The uncertainty of his father's health made it the safest choice for them."

The senator turned toward Jeremy. "How is your father now?"

"Doing very well. My mother has made herself a nervous wreck worrying over him these past several years, but she takes excellent care of him."

"Is her nervousness due to his health or the stress of being in the program?"

Jeremy paused, caught by surprise at how the senator had stripped away the superfluous factors and revealed the heart of the issue. Just like his own father. His lips tugged upward into a quick smile.

"With my mother, it's a little of both."

"I see." Then the senator's gaze went back to Dekker. "How do we make this better for all the Walkers?"

"There isn't much we can do. The current methods were working fine, until—"

"—Abby," the senator finished for him. "You see, Marshal Dekker, she's my first concern. And starting today, she's going to become more of a concern for you. My daughter is the best of young women. She has always put her family first. She considers the impact of her actions and her associations on my political career, this church when she is acting as its agent and on her testimony as a Christian."

Jeremy just sat there, the truth of the senator's words shaming him. He'd been so focused on what he wanted and what would make his life easier. Not once had he stopped to consider how difficult his silence, his hard-hearted lack of cooperation, had made Abby's job. She hadn't asked him to give her all the details. She'd only asked him to define the restrictions he was placing on the project, so she could create a financial plan that included him. She'd been asking him to tell her what rules she needed to obey to give him his dream.

I am an idiot.

And she knew he was, but she'd still tried to help.

"What needs to happen so I can live a real life? One where I don't have to worry about being tracked down and killed if my picture is posted on Facebook. One where I only have to tell a reporter, 'no comment' if I don't want to comment. Where I can go to a Braves game with my best friend without being afraid my face will end up on the jumbotron."

Dekker rolled his wrists to palms up and shrugged. "There is no protocol for that."

"Then there needs to be one." Senator Blackmon's deep voice carried the weight of an edict. He looked away from Dekker and asked Jeremy, "Do you care for my daughter?"

"Yes."

"Then, why are you letting her gallivant all over Atlanta with that basketball player?"

"Sir, I thought your being here today, learning about my family being in witness protection, would be explanation enough."

"Well, it's not. Not where my daughter's concerned." He rose and skewered Jeremy with an accusing glare. "You come clean with her. She deserves to know the truth, so she knows what her options are and can make informed choices about her life."

"But—"

Dekker stood, as well. "With all due respect, Senator, Jeremy can't go around telling people he's in witness protection. It defeats the purpose of living his life under the radar to keep his family safe."

"Then, present me with a solution to this problem that will keep Jeremy and his family safe and let them live their lives like regular people." Before Dekker could form an excuse, he went on, "Find a solution within a month, or I'll take care of it for you."

"Are you threatening to endanger citizens under the protection of the Witness Security Program?"

The senator chuckled under his breath and smiled. "No, I'm promising to free this boy here and his family from the prison you've kept them in all these years." He paused in the doorway. "Dekker, go home and think about how you'd feel having to live your life following that list of rules you keep imposing on the Walkers. How long would it be before you started plotting your escape? You're lucky they've stayed under your thumb this long. I expect an exit strategy in my hands within a month." He closed the door before Dekker could respond.

Dekker paced Jeremy's office, his jaw tense, mashing his fist into the palm of his other hand. "This wouldn't have happened if you hadn't gone and fallen for the one woman who posed a risk to you and your family."

The senator's threat to Dekker was a ray of hope for Jeremy. Dekker had never been willing to budge, but he had no choice now. Whatever happened, it didn't ensure him of a relationship with Abby. But it gave him a chance. Relief and excitement thrummed through his veins.

"Wipe that happy look off your face. You still can't tell her about the program."

Jeremy was in his face. "Why not? Look, Dekker, I have followed every rule you've decreed even when it made my life almost impossible to live. No one should have to drive people away from them on just your say-so."

"No one told you to pick such high-profile friends."

"I have never assessed anyone I've met beyond whether they had a camera and planned to use it to take my picture. The Delaneys and the Blackmons are good Christian people. I'm a minister. They are faithful members of my congregation. Upstanding citizens. One is a US senator. Who would you have me surround myself with?"

Dekker stepped away from him. When he reached the door, he looked back with a smug smile. "You aimed too high, Pastor. I told you to keep it simple. Now, even if you tell dear, sweet Abby the truth, it's too late. She won't forgive you." And closed the door.

The closest thing at hand was the toy basketball on his desk. He flung it at the door, using every ounce of anger Dekker's taunting words kindled to life within him. It ricocheted off the door and took out the lamp on his desk. Jeremy stood there, his breath coming hard and fast. He'd never wanted to destroy something so bad in his life. He stalked out of his office.

Mrs. Hall spoke to him, but he shook his head as he strode by on his way out into the sunlight. He couldn't breathe. The air was hot, the sun blinding. He walked around the church property, studying what God had entrusted to his care. The land, the buildings, the people and this city.

He asked God to take the anger and hurt. To show him how to overcome this burning urge to pound on something. He looked up. On the other side of the tract of grass was the outside court where he and the boys played basketball on Tuesday nights. The day care brought the little ones out here sometimes to play four square. A ball was resting against the base of the goal post. It was as if God was saying, "Go ahead. Pound away."

He jogged over to the ball, digging in his pockets for his keys and a handful of change. He put them down where the ball had rested. With his eyes closed, he pressed the ball between his hands, gauging its firmness. Solid as a rock. He smiled. The feel of the ball, warmed by the sun, leached into his fingers, drawing out the tension and frustration twisting him in knots. He pounded those emotions into the asphalt of the court with each bounce of the ball. He dribbled, doing routes, pivoting, stretching and shooting. Sometimes he had the shot, sometimes the ball bounced away and he hustled to grab it.

After a sideways, over-handed shot from center court, he stopped and whirled around. Shaun Fowler was leaning against the opposite goal post.

"That's some pretty good shooting, Pastor. Something tells me there's a story behind all your skill and the fact that you're doing this instead of out signing autographs or filming a commercial."

Jeremy was soaking wet. Rivers of sweat ran down his face. His shirt stuck to his body better than duct tape. He wiped his brow with the back of his wrist. "I told you, I don't like cameras."

"Yeah, that's what you said. The locals may not be able to appreciate the skill behind the ability they see when you're playing with your community league team, but I'm trained to recognize skill. And you have lots of skill."

"It wouldn't matter now. I'm too old to keep up with the fresh-out-of-college players. But, thanks for the vote of confidence. It means a lot coming from you."

Shaun walked up to him, and Jeremy offered him the ball. He took it, dribbling it on the side while they talked. "Aren't you curious as to what I'm doing here?"

"I could be a jerk and say it's a free country, but I'm really working on being a better person. So, I'll guess that it's either to check on how our church is spending your money, or you came to see Abby and decided to swing by and see how construction was going."

He flashed a bright smile. "Very perceptive. You got the order backwards, though. I was going to check on the construction progress and use it as my excuse to visit Abby."

Jeremy forced his stiff neck to nod his head. "Come on then, I'll show you around."

"It's okay. The general contractor is a friend of mine. He gave me the two-dollar tour. You used our kitchen design. I thought you were buttering me up when you asked me about it."

Jeremy couldn't keep the edge out of his voice. "I don't give false compliments. Your design was cheaper than ours was and offered more functionality. The bank was very happy."

Shaun stepped back, tossing the ball at him. He caught it and passed it back. They spread out, the distance between them growing as they traded shots. A slight breeze stirred, helping dry his shirt.

"So, since you're such an honest man, care to explain why you aren't more than just a friend to the lovely Abby?"

The words dove deep into his chest like a long blade, and just as Shaun threw the ball toward him, he froze. The ball splattered his nose. He leaned back, pinching high on the bridge of his nose, and fought against the sudden wave of nausea that had nothing to do with having his nose smashed by a basketball. Again.

Chapter 8

Shaun rushed forward, gripping Jeremy's shoulder, trying to keep him still. "Hold your head back. Breathe through your mouth. I'm sorry, man. If our positions were reversed, you'd have taken me out by chasing a question like that with a high chest pass."

Jeremy clamped his teeth together to keep from biting his tongue in two. Never again would he ask God to help him get over his urge to pound something. He fought to breathe through his mouth without throwing up. A bloody nose—again.

"Slow breaths. Slow breaths. Tell me which way to the office, and I'll guide you there." Shaun's breathing wasn't so even either.

Using his shirt to staunch the flow of blood, Jeremy

brought his head back to level and waited for the spinning to stop. "I can't believe this."

"Hey, I feel bad enough about this already. You should know to keep your face guarded."

"Are you kidding me?" His voice was muffled through the wadded-up shirt covering most of his face. "My sinuses just recovered from an elbow to the nose during a game last season. Abby..."

"What? You want me to get Abby for you?" Shaun whipped his phone out and slid his finger across the screen before Jeremy got in a second blink.

He tried to stop him, but apparently, she answered "Shaun calls" on the first ring. She'd think he did this on purpose. Then she'd kill him. "Don't tell her. Just hang up," Jeremy tried.

Too late.

Shaun glanced at him as he said, "I'm at the church. Yeah, uh, look, I accidentally—no, we were throwing the ball around, and I think I broke Jeremy's nose. He's bleeding—" Shaun stared at his phone before glancing back at Jeremy. "She hung up." He stood there, alternating his gaze between the phone and Jeremy.

"Yeah, well, I did say not to tell her." He let out a weary sigh. "Let's get inside. I better get some of the blood off my face before she gets here."

"She's coming here?"

"You'll be lucky if she doesn't bring a paramedic with her. She was at the game when the guy popped me in the nose with his elbow. She gets a little crazy at the sight of blood."

"Most women do. They're squealing, and then they

get all light-headed while you're trying to get both eyes to focus in the same direction. And it will be your fault if you don't catch them when they drop. Never mind that you're bleeding."

Jeremy slowly shifted his head around, keeping the shirt against his nose, and shot him an impatient glare. "She doesn't faint. She turns into a growling mama bear. The doctor had to wait over five minutes for her to finish her examination before he could take a look and declare nothing was broken last time."

"I see."

"You will. If you ever get hurt around her, prepare to be smothered with the attorney version of Florence Nightingale."

He pulled a clean shirt from the small closet in the hallway and then settled Shaun in his office.

"What if she gets here before you come back?" Shaun followed him to the door, his eyes a little wild with panic.

The throbbing in his nose was making its way up and across his forehead. He didn't have time for this. "Tell her I'm fine. I went to check on something. But whatever you do, don't give her any details that involve the word *blood*. Okay?"

He nodded, but Jeremy wasn't convinced. He hurried into the church kitchen and grabbed several hand towels and a zipper bag off the supply shelf near the ice machine. In the men's room, he wet one of the towels with warm water, then added soap from the dispenser. He wiped the streaks of blood off his neck and chest. Using another towel, he rinsed the soap from his skin. He did the same with his face, working his way up from his chin and jawline, around his mouth and, finally, to the tender area around his nose. No new streaks appeared. He blew out a thankful breath. Just then, the bathroom door opened, and Shaun poked his head inside.

"Tell me she isn't right behind you."

"She who?" A very authoritative, very mama-bear voice growled from the hall.

Jeremy glanced in the mirror for any stray smudges of red before pulling the white polo on over his head. He needed to put a spare red or black shirt in the closet for next time. Never mind praying there wouldn't be one. He rinsed the towel again, folded it and then gently situated it over his upper lip and the bottom of his nose. Shaun shot him a look of apology as he held the door for him so he could keep the towel-wrapped bag of ice across his nose.

The second he cleared the men's room door, Abby snatched away the hand holding the ice to his face and pushed him toward the wall. Shaun's jaw was hanging loose. Jeremy grimaced and prepared for the smothering.

"What were you thinking? You promised you'd be more careful from now on." She rose on her toes, and he bent at the knees. Her gaze was so penetrating, she might have a clearer image of his nose than any X-ray would reveal.

"We were tossing the ball back and forth. It was a harmless accident. Ow! What'd you do that for?" He reared his head back before she mashed "the spot" again and whacked his skull against the wall. "Ow! Please, stop." He shot Shaun a look. "Tell her I'm fine."

Shaun had recovered from his shock and was trying not to laugh, but his eyes gave him away. "Abby, Jeremy's fine. His nose isn't broken, just bruised."

She positioned herself, so she could see both of them. "How do you know? I read about the dangers of a broken nose. A bone fragment can go right through—"

"Abby," Jeremy howled. "I didn't break my nose. It's just like last time. It wasn't bleeding when I put the ice on it. Now, if the two of you will excuse me, my day was pretty eventful before your boyfriend here tried to take my head off with a basketball." He shouldn't have said it that way, but he'd been guilt-tripped by a US senator, mocked by the US Marshals and accidentally assaulted by an NBA All-Star. He would not stand by and willingly watch Abby break his heart when she picked Mr. Everything over him.

"You can't drive." Abby placed her hand against his chest and pushed him back toward the wall.

"Oh, yes, I can."

Her eyes narrowed. "Let me restate that. You aren't driving yourself home."

He blew out a long breath. "Abby, I'll be fine. I just want to go home and lie down."

"That's exactly what you should do. I'll drive you."

"No," both men said.

She glanced between them. "Why not?"

Shaun looked at Abby for a moment before shaking his head. "I'll take him home."

"No, don't be silly. You have more important things to do than run a taxi service. I'll see to it he gets home."

Jeremy left them arguing over who would play the

chauffeur and walked back to his office. He eased into his chair and leaned his head back, draping the ice pack over his nose. *Ahhh.* The quiet lasted for a few minutes.

"Jeremy, that was rude." Abby stood in front of his desk, her hands on her hips. "Shaun came all this way to see the progress on the center. The least you could have done was tell him goodbye."

"He left?"

"Of course he left." She came around his desk. "Now, let me see your nose."

He removed the ice pack and sat up before she got close enough to inflict any more damage. "See, no blood." He held the other towel up for her inspection.

"Thank the Lord. I was praying the whole way here that you were okay. I could tell something was wrong by the tone of Shaun's voice. And the minute he mentioned a ball, I just knew."

"You just knew?"

She paused, her hands inches from the sides of his face. "He doesn't go to church."

"So?"

"He said he was at the church. This is the only church he's working with. But we weren't scheduled to meet."

"I think it was supposed to be a surprise."

The room was silent save for the sounds of their breathing and the tick of the clock on the wall. Then, Abby wet her lips before meeting his gaze. "I didn't know."

He nodded. "It's okay." Dekker's taunt that he'd already lost her made his stomach burn with churning acid. He blinked against the sting in his eyes.

"Will you let me call Nick to take you home?"

If it meant she'd leave before he gave in and asked her what she wanted with Shaun, he'd agree to anything. He nodded. She picked up the phone on his desk and keyed the number.

"Nick, are you in the office? Great. Can you swing by the church and run Jeremy home? No. He had a bit of an accident. With a basketball. No, Shaun Fowler. He did not hit him on purpose."

Jeremy reached up and took the phone away from her. "Come, get me. I'll explain on the way to my house."

She snatched the phone back, then glared at him when she heard the dial tone.

"What?" he said. "You hung up on Shaun."

"That was different."

"Why, because you did it? Courtesy goes both ways."

"Men," she growled.

"Yes, you'll always need us to reach things on the top shelf in the grocery store. Or for loosening tight lids on jars. The population couldn't survive without us for those very reasons."

She handed him back his ice pack. "Goodbye."

He couldn't smile. No, really, he couldn't. The whole area around his nose was swollen. "I'm sorry. I was teasing. I tease you when I'm not sure what to say."

She stopped at the door. "Why'd you send me flowers?"

"To apologize."

"For what?"

"Do you have time for me to list all the things that

have happened between us lately that warranted an apology bouquet?"

"So it had nothing to do with Shaun?"

He closed his eyes against the ache in the middle of his chest and prayed for strength. "Abby, Shaun is your business. Well, he's a little bit church business, too. But if you've met someone that you want to get to know better, I'm happy for you. You're one of the finest women I know. I just want you to find the man who deserves you."

Her eyes glistened like pools of silver caught in the moonlight before she turned and left.

Abby came into the kitchen through the garage after a long and emotionally draining day. She set her keys and her purse on the granite countertop while she toed off her high heels.

"You're keeping pretty long hours, aren't you?"

She jumped. "Daddy, you scared me."

He was at the breakfast table with stacks of papers all around him. His coffee mug was pushed aside, and he'd set his reading glasses on the open file in front of him. Bringing his mug with him, he walked over to the coffeepot and refreshed his cup. He held the pot up in her direction.

"No, thank you. Were you waiting up for me?"

"I heard you tell your mother you and Gina were going to Katherine's tonight to help her with wedding stuff. I didn't know what time you'd get in, and I didn't want to miss you."

He opened his arms, and she walked into his hug.

"Is Mama feeling better? She sounded better this morning at breakfast."

"She's on the mend. Taking her vitamin C and resting like the doctor said. The cough is almost gone."

"Good. She's been itching to get out in her vegetable garden, and I wanted her to wait."

"Abby, can you sit with me for a few minutes?"

His tone frightened her. Her heart had almost stopped once already today when Shaun had called about Jeremy. "Daddy, is everything okay?"

"Everything's fine." He smiled and guided her to the table, then moved his papers out of their way.

She took the seat across from him. "Then, why did you wait up for me?"

"I wanted to talk to you. How are things going with the recreation center?"

"Everything's right on schedule. The outer walls are getting taller and taller. I can't wait until they get the structure closed in with the roof. It will go so much faster when they don't have to worry about the weather."

"You're enjoying watching God's plan for the church happen."

"Yes, and I'm excited for Jeremy. The summer outreach will be our biggest ever."

He took a sip of coffee. "I was at the church today."

"You were? When?"

"Late morning, right before lunch. I didn't realize how big the building was going to be. But then, I don't get to see it every week, so it should look very different when I do."

His gaze was steady on her. He'd tell her why he was there if he wanted her to know. She couldn't shake the sense of scrutiny in his gaze, as if he were analyzing her every move. "Jeremy insisted we build it large enough to house a full basketball court with bleachers. That was his biggest selling point for the project. The committee voted in favor of all his design recommendations."

"The two of you make a pretty good team."

The slow smile spreading across her face froze. "Not with this project. It's been a lot more demanding than I expected. I recruited Gina to act as my assistant. I'm planning to step down as director of the finance committee when this fiscal year ends."

"Abby, why?"

Did she have to tell him? He should already know. And when Jeremy made it clear her perfect man was out there waiting for her, it was one rebuff too many for her heart. "I need to focus my attention in a new direction."

"When's the last time you spoke with Jeremy?"

"Today."

His gaze shot to hers. She could tell he hadn't expected that. It was nice to be a little unpredictable.

"When?"

"This afternoon. Shaun had stopped by to check out the construction, and apparently he and Jeremy ended up on the basketball court." The more she talked, the more intense his gaze became. "He called and let me know Jeremy got popped in the nose with the ball."

"Is he okay? Did he have to go to the hospital?"

When she shook her head, a piece of hair slipped loose from her clip, and she pushed it behind her ear. "He's fine. By the time I got there, he'd cleaned it up himself, and the bleeding had stopped." She gasped.

"What?"

"He's going to ruin Katherine's wedding photos. Oh, never mind. What am I saying? He'll do anything within his power to get out of having his picture taken." She slammed her palm down on the table. "That dirty rat. If he staged this little 'accident,' I'm going to wring his neck."

"Why would you think he'd purposely take a hit in the face that sounds pretty painful to avoid having his picture taken?"

"Daddy, Jeremy is a true man of God. He cares more for his congregation than any minister I've met. His passion for the youth, especially the boys, and wanting to help them know Christ, fills my heart with joy to watch. But he isn't rational when it comes to even the chance of having his picture taken. So, yes, I truly believe he would walk into a wall if he had to in order to get out being photographed. Even if I used every spot-covering cosmetic on the market, I don't think I could hide all the discoloration under his eyes. Katherine is going to be devastated."

He took her hands in his. "Hey, it's going to be okay. Nick and Katherine's wedding will be perfect. And don't type that letter of resignation to the finance committee just yet."

"Daddy, you—"

"You know what I've always admired about you? Your never-ending flow of patience."

She snorted. "Sorry. I have almost no patience at all."

He winked at her. "Yes, you do. For the important things. And those are the things everyone should have the patience to wait on."

"Are we talking about Jeremy? Is there something you think you know about him that I don't? Because if there is—" she swallowed against the tears trying to clog her throat "—I really need to know he's worth my effort."

"He is. I know things have been strained between you lately, but it's going to get better."

"When?"

"I can't tell you that."

She growled. "If one more man uses those five words as his answer to me, I won't be responsible for my actions." She met his raised eyebrow with one of her own. "Tell me something to hold me. Like a retainer."

"Oh, you are an attorney down to your toes, aren't you?"

"I learned from the best."

"All right. Flattery will gain you a little information. Now, this isn't specific, and you're going to have to trust me when I assure you that soon all your questions about him will be answered to your satisfaction."

"All of them?"

"Well, he won't be able to hide behind the phrase 'I can't' anymore."

Her eyes went wide. "What?"

"His avoidance of cameras isn't a syndrome or a phobia. It's…curable."

"So it is a fear. I knew it. He was so mad when I called him a chicken."

"Abby, you have to stop pushing him about this. He really can't explain it to you." He watched her, looking deep into her eyes. "He isn't allowed to tell you."

They traded earnest looks across the table. His was narrow eyed, as if willing her to see his thoughts. She nibbled on her lower lip, absorbing all he'd shared, stripping away her assumptions and expectations, until she was left with just the words and what they said. "He can't tell me because someone or something won't let him. That's what you're saying?"

He nodded. "And don't ask *me* any more either. I probably shouldn't have told you that much. But I don't like to see you looking so sad." He caressed her cheek with his hand. "Promise me you'll pray every day and ask God to show you what you should do."

"I will." She shook her head. "Sorry, Katherine was chanting 'I will' while we put the reception favors together."

"It's good to stay in practice. You never know."

"Daddy, I need you to promise me something this time." After he met her gaze, she smiled. "I care a lot for Jeremy. But he's kept a distance between us for all the time I've known him. I won't beg any man to love me. If I'm not good enough for him to work hard at winning my love, he isn't the man for me. So, unless he holds me in as high a regard as I hold him, whenever this truth that you think will clear the way for us comes out, all we'll ever be is friends. I want a marriage as happy as yours and Mama's."

"That's exactly what your mama and I want for you. You deserve the very best. And not just because you're my child." He rose and came to her side of the table. After wrapping her in a big hug, he kissed the top of her head. "Good night, honey. I love you."

"I love you, too."

Abby sat alone in the kitchen for a long time. Her emotions had run the gamut today. She'd been terrified that Jeremy was hurt and angry that Shaun may have caused it. They'd talked in the hall before he left the church. He'd kissed her cheek and asked her to promise that if her heart were ever free, she'd call him.

She hadn't understood what he meant at first. Maybe it took a stranger with a new perspective coming in and shaking things up to open her eyes to just how deep her feelings for Jeremy ran. And how transparent her heart was. She prayed her father was right. That Jeremy could break away from whatever was controlling his actions. He deserved the freedom to choose what made him happy.

And it had better be her.

Chapter 9

The day after the Delaney-Harper wedding, Jeremy sat with his parents in their living room, along with Senator Blackmon and Marshal Dekker. It was a large, airy room with walls covered in a honeyed pine paneling from more than a few decades past. But his mom had made the throw pillows for the chairs and the long sofa. His father had stripped the old paint off the rocking chair, coffee table and the side chair and table, and restained them a golden color a shade lighter than the walls.

Dekker got up and stood in front of the brick fireplace. Tension held his body taut even in the "at ease" position he had assumed. His legs were shoulder-width apart, and his arms were clasped behind his back. "What is this stipulation you're putting on whatever action we decide to take to resolve your media presence problem?" His voice dripped with disdain.

"I think it's a little more than a media presence problem, Dekker." Then, just tired of the other man's attitude, Jeremy pushed back. "You'd blame me if a street camera picked me up using facial recognition software."

"Jeremy, let him get it out of his system. If all goes according to plan, this is the last day he can tell you what to do." The senator offered both of them a toothy smile.

Jeremy returned in kind. Dekker sneered.

His dad laughed. "They have your number, don't they, Dekker?"

"I'll still be involved in your lives."

Jeremy's mom came in with a tray full of coffee cups and a carafe and set it on the table in front of the sofa. "Not unless you request a transfer, and I don't see you giving up the change of seasons for a drier climate." She handed him a cup filled with black coffee, then patted his arm.

He mumbled a few times but toned his testiness down after that. "Okay, Senator, what is your idea to turn Walker here into your daughter's Prince Charming?"

The senator glanced at Dekker. "I'd be lying if I said Abby isn't part of the reason I'm interested in Jeremy's situation and the restrictions on his life. But he's also my pastor. A wise and compassionate counselor, despite his youth. And he's my friend. So, yes, I am injecting myself into the way you're handling the Walker family's unique situation."

"Thank you, sir." Jeremy switched his gaze to Dekker. "Can we please wait to put our plan into action until after Nick and Katherine return from their honeymoon? I don't want anything that appears unpleasant to overshadow this time for them. If Nick caught a newscast about me, he and Katherine would be on the next plane home. I don't want that. I've waited this long to get out from under this cloud. I can wait a few more weeks."

"You agreed not to tell Miss Blackmon the details until after the fact," Dekker reminded him.

"And I don't agree. She's an officer of the court. Any conversation they have could be blanketed by privilege, if need be." The senator was sitting next to Jeremy's dad. Apparently, they'd been swapping stories about Dekker's cantankerousness.

Jeremy's dad was nodding and getting more animated the longer he and the senator talked. Jeremy took the opportunity to go speak to his mom. He found her in the kitchen, putting another pot of coffee on to brew. He came up and wrapped his arms around her.

"Goodness, what did you do or what are you about to do that you need to sweeten me up?"

He laughed. "Nothing. I just didn't get to hug you when I came in."

She hit the start button on the coffeemaker, then reached for him. "How do you know this senator?"

"He goes to my church." When the silence grew, he caved. "His daughter is Abby."

"That's Abby Blackmon's father?"

"Yes."

"So, he's really here for her."

"Does it matter? If it means we'll be free of this cloud of paranoia, don't you want that?"

She reached up and laid a gentle hand on his cheek. "I want you to be happy with a family of your own. And if what they decide today makes it possible for you to have that, then, yes, I want that. What happened to your face?"

He ducked out of reach. "Mom, it occurred weeks ago."

"And you didn't go to the doctor, did you?"

"Nothing was broken, and the swelling is gone. The bruise is just taking longer to fade."

"Uh-huh. Did Miss Blackmon offer any TLC?"

"Mom. We aren't having this discussion."

She folded her arms across her chest, "Why not?"

How he got himself into these things, he'd never know. He blew out a long breath. "She gets really upset if someone gets hurt. Especially if there's blood involved."

"Weak—"

"There's nothing weak about Abby. She transforms into a blonde version of you."

She opened her mouth, paused and then closed it again. "I don't know why I shouldn't take that as a compliment, except that somewhere in there I'm positive you were being unflattering about my concern for both your and your father's health."

"See, there was a compliment."

The doorbell rang. He followed his mother down the hall to see who it was. Dekker met them in the hallway. The senator was already turning the knob to open the door.

"Sir, you should—"

By then, the door was open, and standing there, framed by a backdrop of summer sunshine, dressed in bronze tailored slacks and a copper-colored blouse, holding a briefcase, was Abby Blackmon. "Am I late?"

The senator leaned in and kissed her cheek. "Not at all. You're right on time." He stepped back to let her pass.

Dekker surged forward. "Blackmon, I don't know what you think you're doing, but you've made a huge mistake. This is not authorized."

Abby waved a folded piece of paper in front of his face. "This says I am. Now, if you will excuse us, I need a moment alone with my client." She turned to Jeremy.

He was still staring. "What?"

She pushed him down the hall, following his father's beckoning motion until they arrived at the door of the man cave.

"Y'all won't be disturbed in here." As soon as they were far enough inside, he closed the door.

Jeremy backed away until he was at the sofa he usually sat on when he came over to watch games with his dad. "You're not my attorney. I don't have an attorney."

She set her briefcase on the floor. "Jeremy, listen to me. You follow the rules. You don't ever break them. So, we're going to follow the rules. Give me a dollar." She held out her hand.

He plowed his fingers through his hair and paced

back and forth along the length of the sofa. "I don't understand."

"Give me a dollar and I'll explain."

"I don't have a dollar."

"What? Who doesn't have a dollar on them for emergencies?"

He dug in his pocket and pulled out a small wad of papers and business cards. He straightened and pulled papers apart until he found some cash. "I have a five. Will that work for this?"

She cocked her head to the side and studied him for a moment, then nodded. She caught the bill as it arced toward her and put it in her pocket. "You're angry with me."

He walked up to her, his jaw clenched tight. "I don't think you know what you just walked into. And I can't tell you. Which means you're going to be really upset with me, again, because I'll have to give you one or both of your least favorite two-word answers in reply."

She patted his cheek. "The five dollars was my retainer. I am now your attorney. The paper I gave Dekker, right?"

Jeremy nodded. "Marshal Dekker, with the US Marshals Service."

"Ah. That is the first time since I met you that you've told me the truth."

"What? I tell you the truth all the time. I do not lie."

"In court, when a witness is sworn in, they are required to swear to tell, 'the truth, the whole truth, and nothing but the truth.' Do you know why that is?"

He went to the sofa and sat down. Somehow, he

managed to hold on to his manners and motioned her to his father's recliner. She perched on the edge with her hands folded in her lap.

"Who told you?"

"Who told me what?"

"Abby, enough. This isn't a game. It's my parents' lives. It's my life. You can't walk in here, take five dollars and start asking me questions you know I can't answer."

She rose and came to stand in front of him, her hands resting on her hips. "Actually I can. My father talked to your father last week. Mr. Walker expressed some concern for his son's legal rights in a family matter involving a federal agency. So my father assured him that he knew an attorney who would be willing to represent you, for a modest fee. And since Marshal Dekker was going to be here today, I'm here to make sure any demands or stipulations he wants to place on your future don't go beyond the scope of his authority or against your civil rights." She sat down beside him.

"I've lived my life hiding behind a curtain, prowling the fringes of other people's lives like I was a mist or a vapor at the mercy of the wind. I've been conditioned to not tell anyone anything." He turned his head to look at her. "And the one person I wanted to tell everything to for the longest time was you. And I couldn't because I didn't know if I could pay the price. I'm—"

"If you dare finish that sentence with a word that begins with a *c* or an *s*, you'll need Dekker to protect you from me." She rose from her seat.

There was a brief knock, and then his mother came

into the room. "Jeremy, I don't know what's going on between the two of you, but the senator and your father can't keep Dekker at bay much longer. Now hurry up." With her order issued, she walked out, closing the door behind her.

"I take it that was your mother."

"Yes, Delores Walker."

"I like her. She knows how to boss you around."

This was a nightmare. *Lord, please show me what to do.* He stood up. "All right, after we get through whatever happens out there, I will sit down with you, in your office, and you can ask me anything, and I will answer you using as many words per sentence that you want, and they won't include, *I can't* or *I'm sorry.* I promise."

"Okay. Let's go."

In the living room, Dekker had gone beyond pacing to a half-step march around the room. "Senator, you're accusing me of abusing my power. What do you call the circus that just paraded through here claiming attorney-client privilege?"

"Be very careful what else you say. I've told you my reasons for getting involved in this matter. I admire Mr. Walker for doing what he had to in order to keep his family safe when they were threatened. In fact, you should be appreciating the danger an overprotective father, both heavenly and earthly, could pose to you."

With Abby seated next to his mother on the long sofa against the front wall, and the senator and his father sitting in the two swivel rockers, Jeremy moved the wooden, black-lacquered rocking chair nearer to his father.

"Senator, you called this meeting. So, since we're all here now, why don't you tell us why that is?"

He nodded and rose to his feet. "Cliff and Delores are comfortable with most of the restrictions on their lives because they tend to keep more to themselves. The problem is Jeremy and the ineffective way you've handled his need to live a low-profile life. Correct?"

Dekker nodded from his post in front of the cold fireplace.

"Is the threat that caused them to enter witness protection still considered viable against them?"

"Not as imminently as it was at the time. When Mr. Walker had his massive heart attack, he took a leave of absence from his accounting business. He entrusted the day-to-day operations to his business partner, Darius Michaels. Mr. Michaels had some gambling debts that he managed to keep secret from not only Mr. Walker but also his wife and the rest of his family. One of the men he owed several thousands of dollars to needed help creating some financial records to explain the large influx of cash his import-export business was receiving."

Just then, Jeremy's mom stood up and walked to his dad's side. Her first two fingers went automatically to the side of his neck, along his carotid artery. "Cliff, I saw you flexing your fingers. Are you feeling any tingling in your arm?"

He grasped her hand and brought it to his lips. Her face flushed a soft pink. "No, honey, it's fine. Besides, it's the wrong side. I was flexing my fingers to keep from making a fist and to keep my blood pressure down. I can't forgive myself for the dangerous situation I put you and Jeremy in by not knowing what kind of person Darius was. If I had, none—"

"I guess it's my fault you had the heart attack, since I'm the one who has cooked your meals for you all these years."

"Delores, the arteriosclerosis was hereditary. Your care and healthy cooking is what prevented the attack from happening sooner. You saved my life." He squeezed her hand against his lips.

She leaned down and kissed the top of his head. "And you know that, given your health at the time, what you did—what we decided together—was the best thing for us?"

They embraced, and Jeremy looked away. His gaze landed on Abby. She had her lower lip caught between her teeth, and her eyes were shimmering pools of silver. He'd wanted to shield her, protect her from the risk that being around him could bring her. He'd tried to protect her the same way his father had tried to protect his mother and him.

Abby looked over, and her gaze tangled with Jeremy's. When his father had brought his mother's hand to his lips, she'd almost lost it. That's where he learned the charm and chivalry. She was still furious with him for keeping this from her. They could have found a way, somehow, to work around whatever all this was. Because the little update the marshal had just delivered had provided her with the most details she'd received so far.

Her father had been waiting for her last night when she got home late and exhausted from cleaning up after Nick and Katherine's wedding. She smiled at the image of her best friend driving off into the sunset with her Prince Charming. She glanced back at Jeremy and fought the wave of tears trying to fill her eyes. Her father had said he needed her to act as Jeremy's attorney today and had given her this address.

She hadn't known his parents lived so close. They'd never been to church—well, now she understood why. Every Sunday morning he stood in the pulpit, looking out over the congregation. He urged them to be truthful in all their dealings, both publicly and privately. That was his most recurring life lesson. And every time he held silent when she asked him how she could help him with the center, he'd been lying to her.

In a twisted way, it made sense, but still, he'd lied by omission to her. To everyone.

"Daddy, you said you thought you had a solution."

Dekker shot her a look. But when her father straightened, ready to answer her, even Dekker became still, listening. Mrs. Walker had come back over to her seat on the sofa next to her.

"Cliff, I'm sorry, but you and Delores have to die."

"What? Are you crazy?"

The uproar in the room was deafening. Jeremy was in her father's face, and her father was speaking in a quiet, calming voice. She had risen, looking from Jeremy's dad to his mom, not knowing how to excuse her father's ridiculous suggestion. She was stopped by the tiny smile tugging at the corner of Mrs. Walker's mouth. This made no sense. None at all.

Mrs. Walker took her hand and drew her back into her seat. "It's going to be okay. Let your father explain the rest."

Somehow, and Abby would ask him how when they got home, her father calmed Jeremy down enough that he stopped yelling. His urgency was so palpable it crackled around him like an aura of kinetic energy, popping and sparking with each step or motion of his hand. He came and sat on the arm of the couch nearest his mother as if he were her self-appointed protector.

"Let me explain. Cliff and Delores and I have been talking these last few weeks." He glanced at Dekker. "Sorry to have probably broken another one of your rules, but I wasn't holding out much hope you would come up with a viable solution to the problem, and that was unacceptable to the three of us."

"Blackmon, you prance around the senate spouting off about responsibility and honor and morals. Yet, here you are ticking off rule after rule that you have knowingly violated that could have jeopardized the Walkers, or if the right person discovered the connection, your own child."

He nodded once, acknowledging the hit. But then he smiled. "The problem with that is you forgot to issue me a rule book. Besides, Cliff and Delores here are my constituents. I have a sworn duty to offer the people I represent in Washington help in resolving their problems when they involve the government. That is why they voted for me."

Jeremy was shaking his head. Abby and Mrs. Walker were squeezing each other's hands and pressing their lips together to keep from laughing. It wouldn't be fair to Dekker. He was so earnest and diligent in his job, but he'd blocked out everything in life that didn't pertain to his rule book.

"Delores has trouble with her knees. She was a nurse, and all those years of long hours standing on her feet have caught up with her. She's going to need a knee replacement soon. Plus all this low-profile living you insist on has made them into hermits. They'd like to travel, make some friends and just relax."

"Wouldn't we all?" Dekker glanced at the senior Walkers. "I guess the three of you have come up with a spectacular idea as to how we can make all this happen?"

"Actually, we have." Mr. Walker joined the discussion. "That place you always threatened to relocate us to out West. We want to go."

"I didn't threaten—" A quick glance at the firm set of Jeremy's jaw and his clenched fists convinced Dekker to stop talking.

"The reason we have to arrange their deaths is because the members of the church know Jeremy's parents are alive. If he suddenly doesn't mention them anymore, that would be suspicious. Plus, he was young enough that the threat was always associated with Cliff. If Cliff and Delores go away in a very public way, the risk to Jeremy drops to the point that stepping outside during a lightning storm is a bigger danger than the people Mr. Michaels was involved with."

"If we fake their deaths, there will be a funeral." This was the first time Jeremy had said anything since her father had suggested they kill his parents—in a fake accident.

Her father came to stand beside him and dropped his hand on his shoulder. "I know. But if we have them cremated or do a closed-casket service, that shouldn't be a problem."

"You want me to get up in front of the church, our church, and tell the membership that my parents were killed in a car accident when they're really living in the middle of Yosemite National Park or something. You want me to lie."

"It would work." Dekker was giving it some thought.

Abby didn't know if she was glad or outraged. "Jeremy, haven't you been doing almost the same thing all these years?"

He turned to face her. "No, Abby. I have told what I was allowed to tell, and I've not answered questions, but I have never looked someone in the face and told them an outright lie. And the parts I had to leave out were done that way to save two people's lives. I don't think God would hold that against me, despite the fact that you do."

"Jeremy, I know this is shocking, and maybe we should have approached you about it before this open discussion—"

"Yeah, Mom. Here you are deciding my life again for me. Only this time, I'm the only one people are going to be looking at as if he's a fraud. Why would anyone heed a single word I say in a sermon?"

"I think all of us have our tempers running a little high to try discussing this any further right now."

Jeremy stood. "No, we resolve this today. I still want to wait until Nick and Katherine are back from their trip to do anything, but I want the plan laid out today. Dekker, you and my parents can work on the particulars. I will stand in front of my church one time and tell them that I've lost my parents. I won't tell them that you're dead. That you died. I will tell them I still feel you alive in my heart. And we have to work out how we will be able to contact each other." He walked toward Dekker and met him toe to toe. "And we will be able to contact each other, or I will give the local newspaper reporter the story he wants so he can win a Pulitzer. Do I make myself clear? It isn't so fun when someone else tells you what to do and you have no choice but to smile and wave, is it?"

"Jeremy." He turned at Abby's touch to his sleeve. "We can talk about it and do it in a way that is the least uncomfortable for you."

The left side of his mouth lifted in a wry grin. "Isn't that what you told me when I refused to do any interviews?"

She nodded. "And see how well that project is going? The outer walls are almost halfway up."

His grin dropped. "And you met Shaun."

Chapter 10

Jeremy and Abby went to meet Nick and Katherine at the airport when they returned from their honeymoon. Nick had left the keys to his SUV for Jeremy to use when he picked them up, so there'd be enough room for their luggage and them to ride home.

"Are you sure, Jeremy?" Abby asked him as they waited in the baggage claim area.

"They're both attorneys. I can do the same thing with them that you had me do. I'm tired of people thinking I'm a freak and not being able to explain that I'm not."

"I understand the reason, and I totally agree. I was asking more about your timing."

His eyes were gritty from the nights of staring at the ceiling, searching his mind for scriptures to support the need for the deception. He had almost found peace with the plan, but until it was implemented, he was caught between two worlds. The one where Abby knew the truth and no one else did. So, nothing was different yet. The rules still applied. No photos, no interviews. No life.

Abby had encouraged him to go through with the plan, but she still considered the fact that he didn't confide in her a lie of omission. And yet she'd come up with the best idea of how to make it more agreeable to him about the church. She and her father had taken Dekker with them to a meeting of elders in the church. It was a private meeting at the Blackmons' residence. It had been put out that they were having a party, but each member on the guest list had received a personal phone invitation from the senator himself.

After everyone had arrived, it was announced that they had a very private matter to discuss involving the church. Dekker had explained the need for them to all sign a form affirming they would never repeat any of the information discussed in the meeting to anyone, either among themselves or to their spouses. The men agreed and even offered to host a memorial service at the church. And went so far as to want to have a plaque erected in the new recreation center in honor of Mr. and Mrs. Clifford Walker. Jeremy had been touched by their support and acceptance of what they had been told.

The next Sunday after the meeting, all the elders had waited inside the sanctuary until they were the last to leave. As each one had come up to Jeremy, he had shaken his hand and told him what a fine man of God he was. It had been the sign he'd needed to accept that this was really happening and that God was not condemning him for the necessary deception. Just like the woman who hid the spies for Israel.

When the newlyweds came out of baggage claim, Katherine ran straight into Abby's arms. They were still laughing, hugging and gesturing when Nick made a slower and much more encumbered appearance. Jeremy transferred the carry-on from Nick's shoulder to his. And then took over the pull handle of one of the sets of larger bags, which were strapped together.

"Well, you're looking all tanned and relaxed."

"I have to say, married life agrees with me so far. So what's been going on while we were away?"

"All kinds of things. Come on, I'll buy you dinner and tell you all about it."

Nick stopped walking. "Wait, when have you ever said you would tell anyone all of anything?" He grasped Jeremy's forearm. "What happened?"

"Nothing I can talk about until I've hired you."

"You got arrested!"

The volume of Nick's explosion earned them a full audience. Several people nearby stopped walking and looked their way. Abby let go of Katherine and came back to him. Her eyes were as big as the giant hoop earrings dangling from her ears.

"Nick, I'm so glad you're home." Then she stepped closer to him, and he bent his head toward her.

When he stepped back, he was looking at Jeremy with a cross-examination stare. Great. He'd be buying him a steak dinner and having to give him a twenty instead of the five that had earned him Abby's legal representation.

"The car's this way." Jeremy readjusted the shoulder strap on the bag and started wheeling the roller bag toward the correct exit.

With all the luggage loaded, Jeremy offered Nick his keys. "Nope, you can drive. That way I don't have to worry about my reaction to whatever you're going to tell me right after you give me a dollar."

Jeremy reached into his front shirt pocket, then extended his first two fingers toward Nick with a twenty tri-folded between them. "I need to hire you both."

Nick snatched the money and held the door for Katherine to climb in the back first. Jeremy reached for the back door on the other side for Abby.

"Uh-uh. She can ride up front. Something tells me I'm going to need the support of my wife to hear this."

Jeremy shook his head, walked around to the front passenger door and held it for Abby. She paused before climbing in and grasped his arm. "You were right. Now is better."

Her agreement was some comfort as he got behind the wheel and cranked the engine. He backed out of the parking space and followed the arrows painted on the floor of the parking garage until they drove up to the tollbooth. He swiped his debit card and handed Nick the receipt.

Once they were merging with traffic on the interstate, Nick leaned forward. "We're clear, we've been retained and you need to start talking."

He glanced up in the rearview mirror and caught

the rigid set of Nick's features. Katherine sat in the middle seat, her head resting on Nick's shoulder. He let out a low sigh.

"The reason I can't have my picture taken or my name in the paper is because my family's in witness protection."

"What? Is your father some sort of mob hit man or something?"

"Hey, do you want me to tell you this, or are you going to try to act it out as if it were a reality TV show?"

Abby reached her hand out, and he looked down at it, then back at her before focusing on the road again. She let her hand drop to the seat. Yeah, the backseat was for true love. The front seat was for separate realities. Sharing his secret was supposed to be freeing. Well, it had been. It had freed him right up from Abby, except for any legal entanglements he might encounter while his life hung in limbo.

"Sorry, just not what I would have guessed. Ever." Nick draped his arm around Katherine.

"Me, neither. When I was seventeen, my father was a partner in an accounting firm. There's a long history of bad hearts on my father's side of the family. With all the care and precautions my mom took over the years with his diet and exercise, he still had a massive heart attack. The doctor ordered him home and with no stress for three months. His partner had a gambling problem."

"Oh, I can guess."

"He was filtering dirty money through some of the firm's accounts for a price. Apparently, he gave himself a raise without upper management of the group he was laundering for approving the increase. Their idea of terminating your employment includes a retirement box buried six feet under."

"People tried to kill your dad?"

"No, no. Nothing like that. My dad couldn't have any stress. All of this happened while he was either in the hospital or at home. But the FBI knocked on our door the night Darius was killed and asked my father if Darius had ever given him anything to keep for him. And he had. The feds knew our situation and about my father's health. So, to save him some stress, they offered to make out like the evidence was found somewhere else, so it kept my dad's name out of everything."

They pulled up to the restaurant but stayed in the car with the engine running. Jeremy unhooked his seat belt and turned around enough that he could see Nick and Katherine better. Abby did the same. Nick and Katherine had unfastened theirs and were now sitting side by side from knee to shoulder. Jeremy shook his head.

"I'm sorry we're hitting you with this before you get home and unpack. But the Marshals wants this done, now that the senator and my dad have worked out the plan."

"Senator Blackmon and your father came up with what plan?"

"They're going to stage a bad car accident and fake my parents' deaths. The elders of the church are holding a memorial service on Friday."

Nick looked at Katherine, then at Jeremy. "Back this

thing up and get on the road. Hit a drive-through with some good food, and we can eat at our house while you give us the millions of details you've left out so far."

So with the plan in place and the truth spread out on the table between them a little while later, Jeremy looked Nick in the eye. "I'm sorry I couldn't tell you. I wanted to, but Dekker, the marshal, has this book of rules, and no photos, no interviews, and tell no one are all part of number one on his list."

"Dude, this is insane. Well, at least we know you're not a chicken. You're the Phantom of Pemberly, living in the shadows, one shot from a camera flash and it's lights out for you."

"You're not mad?"

"No, you weren't even an adult at the time it happened. You had to do what you had to so your family was safe. Thank you for telling me when you were able to, though. That means a lot to me. Do they really have to kill your parents?"

Abby stood up from the table, collecting paper plates, food bags and plastic cups. Katherine helped her, and they walked into the kitchen together.

"Okay, I know my childhood was traumatizing when I was younger. But hearing this tonight, you don't know how many things it explains for me about him. He was so angry when I met him in college. He sat in the corner snarling at everyone, and I could see this lost look in his eyes. I knew what it was because I'd seen it every morning in the mirror until God brought Alice, my mom, into my life."

"How? What happened?"

"He was being a real jerk in Psychology 101. And this teacher liked to use us in experiments on human behavior. He had Jeremy and me stand in front of the class, facing each other. He asked Jeremy what he thought he could do to hurt me. Jeremy got this smirk on his face, and called me Orphan Annie."

Abby gasped. "That's—that's so cruel."

Kat shrugged. "He didn't know. But once he saw the look on my face, he reached out to try to comfort me. I was devastated. I ran out of the class crying. I went to the bathroom and stayed there for two hours. When I came out, he was sitting on the floor, his back against the wall, staring at the door. He got up, offered me his hand in an old-fashioned handshake, and I took it. He said he had called me that because of my hair. He thought that's what mean guys called all girls with red hair, and that it would make me mad. That he didn't know I was an orphan."

They sat down at the counter in the kitchen. Katherine hugged Abby again.

"I told him I wasn't an orphan anymore. God was my heavenly Father, and He had found me a mother."

Abby was laughing and crying at the same time, not able to stop doing either one. "That's when he decided to become a minister, isn't it?"

"Well, I don't know if that was the only influence, but we started volunteering at Grace Community together, and once my major in junior college branched off into pre-law, his shifted to religious studies. After he earned his bachelor's, he went to seminary. So, somewhere in there."

The men joined them in the kitchen, and they had coffee and went over what to expect at the memorial service.

"And you're going to be okay with this minister doing a eulogy?" Nick asked Jeremy.

"He is a minister, but he works with the Marshals sometimes on different things. They thought he would be a good fit for our situation."

Katherine gave him a hug. "So, you get your life back."

"Yep. I will be parentless, but we picked up some new missionaries in California that will be writing us progress reports a lot."

"Ah, that's how they're doing it."

Jeremy grinned. "I don't know what you're talking about. I'm as forthcoming as George Washington. If I cut a tree down, I will own up to it."

Abby was quiet after that. He had accepted this next phase in gaining his freedom, and he didn't show any hesitation about what they were going to be doing. He hadn't told her he was sorry since she'd learned the whole truth. Which meant all the *sorry*s before weren't real. They were part of his cover. But his life was no longer covert.

Jeremy drove Abby home. When he pulled up in front of her house, he said, "Abby, this week is going to be strange. Especially the memorial service. You've been great through all of this. If I'd had any idea that

Dekker was overstepping his authority, I would have hired you sooner."

"And that's the only reason you would have told me, isn't it?"

"What? Abby, don't start. You have no idea what it's been like living under this weight. And now I can see the light at the end of the tunnel, and I'm going to be free. I haven't asked myself what I want, what is my heart's greatest desire, but I will. Because now I can go after it."

And with those words, he told her more than he would ever realize he'd said. He never thought he'd been untruthful with her. She leaned over and kissed his cheek. "I hope you get everything that will make you happy. Goodbye, Jeremy."

She got out of the car and went inside. She shook her head at her father when he stopped her in the kitchen. "No more, Daddy. We're done. I'm done."

Chapter 11

"You lied to me, Jeremy," Abby accused. The memorial service was over. The doors to the sanctuary were closed, shrouding them in privacy.

"No, I didn't."

"You certainly didn't tell me the truth."

"That doesn't mean I lied." Jeremy rose, too incensed by her accusations to stay seated.

Abby crossed her arms across her middle and glared at him. "Oh, please. You're a minister. You know better than anyone there isn't a gray area when telling the truth. Either you do or you don't lie."

"I told you the truth—"

She cut him off. "You said you couldn't tell me."

"That was the truth!" Jeremy's voice echoed throughout the room, rising to match his frustration.

With an unladylike snort, Abby rolled her eyes.

"I told you as much as I was allowed to tell you. Believe me, I wanted to tell you everything."

"That's the problem, Jeremy."

"What is?" A band tightened around his chest.

Abby straightened her shoulders and drew herself as tall as her stilettos allowed. "I don't think I can believe you." Her words were but a whisper in the room.

The glassy sheen in her eyes when her gaze met his was almost his undoing. Her doubt shot a searing pain through the pit of his stomach, but he had to be sure—had to know if all hope was gone. He stepped closer. "Abby, I would never lie to you or anyone. I wanted to tell you. But the Marshals Service's rules didn't allow it. Can't you see? I was trapped between what I wanted to do and what I couldn't."

"If I mattered to you, you would have trusted me and told me anyway."

"If you mattered?" His body was on fire. Outrage that she only saw a piece of the truth heated his blood, making his head pound with the pulsing of his heart. He turned her toward him. "I'm a minister. I have to follow all the rules. I have to set the example for the church. If I don't obey man's law, how can I expect the members to believe God's commandments are sacred and that they should follow them? Do you have any idea how many hours I spent on my knees in agony over having to keep you at arm's length, withholding so much of myself from you? Do you?"

Abby laid her soft hand against his cheek, cradling his jaw. "I've admired you and the burden you carry for your congregation so much that I think I've sort of put you up on a pedestal. It makes your role in real life, among us lesser mortals, harder to accept. Maybe I am judging you too harshly, but you deceived me, Jeremy. Whether on purpose or not. You let me worry and believe things that weren't true. And all I can think is that if I mattered as much as you say, nothing would have stopped you from telling me."

The icy claws of fear were cooling the heat of his anger, thickening his blood to slush, slowing it down. He was losing her. He'd let so many dreams go, at peace with the action in the past, knowing God had a different road, a better purpose for his life. He'd never thought himself worthy of Abby. And maybe he wasn't. Maybe this was God's way of showing him how wrong he'd gotten everything involving her.

"There was no deceit—just not full disclosure."

"I expected more from you. You have always sought God's direction. It elevated you in my eyes." Her voice was hollow, as if coming from someone worn down, weakened by a long fight against a foe she couldn't defeat.

"Maybe that's the problem. You've put me on this dais above everyone else where I'm supposed to live my life, making all the perfect decisions, because I'm a man of God. There's no way I could make a mistake or have a misunderstanding. Abby, you forget, I'm just a man. As fallible as others, if not more so, because everything I do is done under so much scrutiny. I don't know what else I can say to convince you that I never meant to mislead you or hurt you. Hurting you is the last thing I would ever do." He took her hand, kissing her knuckles.

The glassy pale blue of her eyes darkened, and she snatched her hand free. "You think I raised you up too high? What do you call all that nonsense you were spouting at me about how Shaun was the perfect man for me? That he would be able to give me what I wanted, what I deserve."

"I had the best of intentions when I encouraged you to give him a chance."

She turned away, letting out a feral groan before swinging back to face him. "I don't think someone who has lived his life hiding from cameras and anything brighter than a sixty-watt bulb can even begin to understand what I deserve—what I need! What I want."

He reached out but paused with his hands lingering near her upper arms, unsure if she would welcome his touch but wanting so much to soothe her, give her some sort of comfort if he was able. "I'm sorry. I would never presume to know what you want or need. I have no right. But I believe you deserve the world, and it wasn't in my power to give it to you. I thought Shaun could."

Abby stared at him, her face etched in even more anguish, if that were possible. "You really don't know what you're saying, do you? You've asked God to help you build the recreation center, to give you a way out of witness protection and its rules. Did you ask Him to give me the world? Did you ever ask God to give me what I needed? Did you stop to think that God knew exactly what I needed, and all this was meant to do just that? That maybe He knew what you needed, too?"

"I don't understand."

"Of course you don't. If you took all this wisdom and knowledge you think you have about me, what is the one thing—the one thing—I need that I don't already have?"

"I don't know." He held his hands up in supplication.

The hurt in her eyes nearly brought him to his knees. "Then I suggest you pray and ask God to show you what He knows I need. And see what you can do about making that happen."

He stood there, watching what he wanted more than anything in this world walk away, unsure what to say to bring her back. Or if he should. He took a seat in the far back corner of the sanctuary. He closed his eyes, not knowing what to pray. It had been a long time since he'd been this lost, frightened of what lay ahead, questioning where to step next. His prayer was internal. His heart cried out its hurt and confusion, trusting that God knew what Jeremy needed in the same way He knew what Abby needed.

Confessing his fear of losing her gave him a sense of ease that was even more confusing. But by admitting his lack, he was claiming God's capability. Was it wrong to ask God to make a way for him to be with Abby? That was the desire of his heart. What he wanted more than anything else in this world.

The soloist and pianist for Sunday came in to practice. He stayed in the shadows, needing to hear some encouragement. The piano sounded, and he smiled. He knew this song. It was new but very popular. As the soloist sang, the words wrapped around him, holding him in his seat. Each line, each stanza, wrote its truth on his heart, opening his eyes to the meaning of the words.

He was an idiot. He looked down at his hands. God had given him exactly what Abby needed. And both she and God had been waiting for him to open his eyes to the reality that the power lay within him, literally. She loved him. His uncertainty and doubt had kept him from seeing—believing—he could give her what she wanted. But God knew. He'd seen how the pieces of the puzzle fit and knew it would come to this.

Jeremy shot to his feet, digging in his pocket for his keys. He had to find her. He needed to tell her. To show her. To give her what she wanted.

God, show me where she is. He jumped in his car and cranked the volume on the song playing on the radio. The soloist inside had been singing the same one. He laughingly rejoiced in the affirmation. He sang along with the radio. He was going after the woman he loved.

She would be with Katherine. He sped up and changed lanes in front of a slower car. The driver honked. Jeremy just smiled and waved. This was their time. Nothing was going to stand in his way.

He parked in the office parking lot. He was jogging toward the entrance door when he met up with Gina and Toby Hendricks. Jeremy met Gina's curious gaze. "Where is she?"

"Katherine?" Gina shifted the purse on her shoulder.

He hit her with a minister-worthy scowl. "Abby."

Gina's eyes strayed toward the glass doors she'd just exited before snapping back to his. "Um, I think they were having a private conference and didn't want to be disturb—"

Without another word, he moved past her in a rush, shooting through the glass entrance door and around the reception area, aiming for the first office on the right. He opened the door. Both women looked up from the small sofa on the far side of the room. Katherine had her arm draped around Abby, holding her close.

He stopped dead at the sight of Abby crying, huge tears running down her cheeks.

Katherine stood and came toward him wearing her battle glare, as though she could singe a hole right through him. "You have some nerve."

"Yes, I do. But now isn't the time, Katherine." He took her by the arm, assisted her toward the door, pushed her out into the hall and then closed the door in her face.

And locked it.

She yelled through the wooden barrier. "Jeremy, you've hurt her enough. Don't—"

Katherine's words stalled him, the shame of the needless pain he'd caused the woman he loved. But that's why he was here. "Katherine, I know exactly what I've done, and I'm trying to fix it. Just give me a few minutes in here. I'll leave if Abby asks me to."

One final avowal permeated the door. "If one more tear falls from her eyes, you're toast, minister or not."

If he didn't get this right, he wouldn't care what Katherine or Nick or anyone did to him.

Abby rose, wrapping her arms around her middle. "What? Why are you here?" Her voice was thick and raspy.

Jeremy approached her slowly, as if she were a skittish horse. "I need to talk to you."

She drew her lower lip between her teeth before releasing it. "I think we said all there was to say earlier."

He shook his head, stopping in front of her. Close enough to touch. To hold. With a gentle slide of his thumb, he wiped a tear from her cheek. "I caused this. I'm sorry. I promise to do my best to never make you cry again."

"Jeremy—"

With his thumb still damp with her tear, he touched her lips. "Shh. Let me do this. Please. I need to do this. For us."

She tried to speak, but he traded his thumb for his index finger, holding it gently against the swell of her warm lips. Abby's breath trembled, but she nodded.

Jeremy motioned her back to the sofa before dropping to his knees in front of her. He took her hands in his, rubbing his thumbs across the back of them then meeting her questioning gaze. "I've spent the past fourteen years avoiding camera flashes and video cameras. I assess a room for possible media risks before I release my grip on the doorknob. The first time I saw you, a man with a camera called your name, and you turned with a ready smile and let him photograph you. The picture was on the front page of the *Sentinel* the next morning. I knew then I was in trouble."

She shifted on the sofa but stayed silent, waiting for him to go on. He lifted her hands, kissed her knuckles and then, turning them over, placed a kiss in each of her palms. "You were the most beautiful woman I had ever seen. I think I can understand the temptation David felt upon seeing Bathsheba. Except, what kept me from you were the rules of witness protection that were maintaining my parents' safety. That's the only risk I couldn't take to be near you."

"Jeremy," she began.

"No. Let me say all this. I have to, so it's behind us."

She nodded.

He still held her hands but rotated them until their fingers were laced together, woven like the threads in a piece of fabric. "When Shaun showed up, I let the old resentment and some new jealousies take root, and I blamed you. That was wrong. You were doing what you'd been asked to do, and doing it well—without me. That part was the hardest for me to accept. Here you were, so beautiful, warm and kind, with a friendly rapport with the media, and when my limitations held you back from following God's will, you found another way to be obedient. Shaun represented everything I used to want to be. I see now that I have a greater impact than I ever could have had if my life had followed the path I thought I should have traveled. Please, forgive me for being so horrible to you."

"I do. I didn't understand why you were jealous. God helped me see that's what it was. But every time I thought we were getting closer, you would back away, putting even more distance between us than there had been before."

"I know. I was afraid. I wanted everything for you. I wanted to give it to you, and I knew I couldn't. I knew

I would never be part of your world, and I couldn't change anything."

"Jere—"

He squeezed her hands. "I'm almost done. I thought you deserved the world. I thought that's what you needed to be happy. To feel loved. But I really listened to what you said today. I was praying about it, asking God to help me because I didn't know what to do or think. All I knew was I was losing you. And I didn't want that."

Her fingers skimmed his cheek, his jaw, and she looked deep into his eyes. "What's changed?"

He smiled. "I figured out what you want." He cradled her face in his hands, resting his forehead against hers. "It's yours forever—I'm yours forever, if you'll have me."

She drew a shaky breath, closing her eyes slowly, and then exhaled softly.

He continued, "I love you. I love your kindness. Your smile. The way you slide your hair behind your ear when it comes loose from your clip instead of redoing it. The way you care for others. How your gentleness helps people feel better about themselves."

"But—"

He brought his hand to the softness of her cheek and slid that errant strand of hair into place behind her ear. He cupped the back of her head, as he leaned in until he could breathe in the rapid gasps from her lips. "I give you my heart, now and forever. I love you with all I am and all I have."

This godly man, this protector of his family at the cost of his heart—his life. This frustrating, charming, gentle man, her perfect mate, designed by God, was here, at her feet, offering her all she'd ever wanted and more.

She leaned that tiny bit forward, bringing their lips together. The heat of his mouth warmed her to her soul. He leaned up, wrapping his arms around her, drawing her close, as he rained kisses across her brow, her temples and her nose. She sighed and held him more tightly. "I love you, too. But I hope you meant what you said, because once Katherine gets her office back, she's going to call a judge, a senator and a councilman and have charges brought against you."

He tried to pull away. "You don't—"

She rubbed her fingers against his lips. "Shh. My turn." He nipped at her fingertips, and she laughed. "As your attorney and, knowing your unwavering belief in obeying the law to its fullest—"

"Abby," he groaned, trying to pull her close again.

She caught her lower lip between her teeth, and he stopped trying to talk. He couldn't take his eyes off her lips.

"The only way to be absolutely sure I can't be compelled to testify against you is if you're my husband. So, for your protection from civil and federal and senatorial dangers, you should say yes, right now."

He captured her face with his hands, lowering his head until his lips were just above hers. And when he spoke that sweet little word, it slid across her lips, where he sealed it with his kiss.

The rattling of the door handle was their warning. "Katherine's com—"

"Mmm-hmm." He claimed her lips again.

His tender kiss spoke to her heart, promising her forever, finally showing her how much he adored her.

The clapping and whistles from the doorway drew them apart. Gina and Katherine were smiling. Toby had his camera aimed at them.

Jeremy grinned, but he didn't let her go. His embrace was tender but unbreakable. And in a grand style worthy of the front page of the *Sentinel*, he assumed the proper position on bended knee. "Abby Blackmon, will you let me be your everything, just as you're mine?"

She was nodding and crying, and Katherine and Gina were hugging both of them. Jeremy kept her close, not that she had any interest in being anywhere else. Her heart had never been so full. *This* was what she'd asked God to give her. Their gazes met. They moved as one, drawing each other nearer until his lips brushed and held hers in a timeless moment of thankfulness for this blessing from God just for them—each other, now and forever.

* * * * *

REQUEST YOUR FREE BOOKS!

2 FREE INSPIRATIONAL NOVELS
PLUS 2
FREE
MYSTERY GIFTS

Love Inspired

YES! Please send me 2 FREE Love Inspired® novels and my 2 FREE mystery gifts (gifts are worth about $10). After receiving them, if I don't wish to receive any more books, I can return the shipping statement marked "cancel." If I don't cancel, I will receive 6 brand-new novels every month and be billed just $4.74 per book in the U.S. or $5.24 per book in Canada. That's a savings of at least 21% off the cover price. It's quite a bargain! Shipping and handling is just 50¢ per book in the U.S. and 75¢ per book in Canada.* I understand that accepting the 2 free books and gifts places me under no obligation to buy anything. I can always return a shipment and cancel at any time. Even if I never buy another book, the two free books and gifts are mine to keep forever.

105/305 IDN F49N

Name _____ (PLEASE PRINT)

Address _____ Apt. #

City _____ State/Prov. _____ Zip/Postal Code

Signature (if under 18, a parent or guardian must sign)

Mail to the **Harlequin® Reader Service:**
IN U.S.A.: P.O. Box 1867, Buffalo, NY 14240-1867
IN CANADA: P.O. Box 609, Fort Erie, Ontario L2A 5X3

**Are you a subscriber to Love Inspired books
and want to receive the larger-print edition?
Call 1-800-873-8635 or visit www.ReaderService.com.**

* Terms and prices subject to change without notice. Prices do not include applicable taxes. Sales tax applicable in N.Y. Canadian residents will be charged applicable taxes. Offer not valid in Quebec. This offer is limited to one order per household. Not valid for current subscribers to Love Inspired books. All orders subject to credit approval. Credit or debit balances in a customer's account(s) may be offset by any other outstanding balance owed by or to the customer. Please allow 4 to 6 weeks for delivery. Offer available while quantities last.

Your Privacy—The Harlequin® Reader Service is committed to protecting your privacy. Our Privacy Policy is available online at www.ReaderService.com or upon request from the Harlequin Reader Service.
We make a portion of our mailing list available to reputable third parties that offer products we believe may interest you. If you prefer that we not exchange your name with third parties, or if you wish to clarify or modify your communication preferences, please visit us at www.ReaderService.com/consumerschoice or write to us at Harlequin Reader Service Preference Service, P.O. Box 9062, Buffalo, NY 14269. Include your complete name and address.

LIDIR13R

REQUEST YOUR FREE BOOKS!

2 FREE INSPIRATIONAL NOVELS
PLUS 2
FREE
MYSTERY GIFTS

Love Inspired.
HISTORICAL
INSPIRATIONAL HISTORICAL ROMANCE

YES! Please send me 2 FREE Love Inspired® Historical novels and my 2 FREE mystery gifts (gifts are worth about $10). After receiving them, if I don't wish to receive any more books, I can return the shipping statement marked "cancel." If I don't cancel, I will receive 4 brand-new novels every month and be billed just $4.74 per book in the U.S. or $5.24 per book in Canada. That's a savings of at least 21% off the cover price. It's quite a bargain! Shipping and handling is just 50¢ per book in the U.S. and 75¢ per book in Canada.* I understand that accepting the 2 free books and gifts places me under no obligation to buy anything. I can always return a shipment and cancel at any time. Even if I never buy another book, the two free books and gifts are mine to keep forever.

102/302 IDN F5CY

Name _____ (PLEASE PRINT)

Address _____ Apt. #

City _____ State/Prov. _____ Zip/Postal Code

Signature (if under 18, a parent or guardian must sign)

Mail to the Harlequin® Reader Service:
IN U.S.A.: P.O. Box 1867, Buffalo, NY 14240-1867
IN CANADA: P.O. Box 609, Fort Erie, Ontario L2A 5X3

Want to try two free books from another series?
Call 1-800-873-8635 or visit www.ReaderService.com.

* Terms and prices subject to change without notice. Prices do not include applicable taxes. Sales tax applicable in N.Y. Canadian residents will be charged applicable taxes. Offer not valid in Quebec. This offer is limited to one order per household. Not valid for current subscribers to Love Inspired Historical books. All orders subject to credit approval. Credit or debit balances in a customer's account(s) may be offset by any other outstanding balance owed by or to the customer. Please allow 4 to 6 weeks for delivery. Offer available while quantities last.

Your Privacy—The Harlequin® Reader Service is committed to protecting your privacy. Our Privacy Policy is available online at www.ReaderService.com or upon request from the Harlequin Reader Service.

We make a portion of our mailing list available to reputable third parties that offer products we believe may interest you. If you prefer that we not exchange your name with third parties, or if you wish to clarify or modify your communication preferences, please visit us at www.ReaderService.com/consumerschoice or write to us at Harlequin Reader Service Preference Service, P.O. Box 9062, Buffalo, NY 14269. Include your complete name and address.

LIHDIR13R

REQUEST YOUR FREE BOOKS!
2 FREE RIVETING INSPIRATIONAL NOVELS
PLUS 2 FREE MYSTERY GIFTS

YES! Please send me 2 FREE Love Inspired® Suspense novels and my 2 FREE mystery gifts (gifts are worth about $10). After receiving them, if I don't wish to receive any more books, I can return the shipping statement marked "cancel." If I don't cancel, I will receive 4 brand-new novels every month and be billed just $4.74 per book in the U.S. or $5.24 per book in Canada. That's a savings of at least 21% off the cover price. It's quite a bargain! Shipping and handling is just 50¢ per book in the U.S. and 75¢ per book in Canada.* I understand that accepting the 2 free books and gifts places me under no obligation to buy anything. I can always return a shipment and cancel at any time. Even if I never buy another book, the two free books and gifts are mine to keep forever.

123/323 IDN F5AN

Name	(PLEASE PRINT)	
Address		Apt. #
City	State/Prov.	Zip/Postal Code
Signature (if under 18, a parent or guardian must sign)		

Mail to the **Harlequin® Reader Service:**
IN U.S.A.: P.O. Box 1867, Buffalo, NY 14240-1867
IN CANADA: P.O. Box 609, Fort Erie, Ontario L2A 5X3

**Are you a current subscriber to Love Inspired Suspense books and want to receive the larger-print edition?
Call 1-800-873-8635 or visit www.ReaderService.com.**

* Terms and prices subject to change without notice. Prices do not include applicable taxes. Sales tax applicable in N.Y. Canadian residents will be charged applicable taxes. Offer not valid in Quebec. This offer is limited to one order per household. Not valid for current subscribers to Love Inspired Suspense books. All orders subject to credit approval. Credit or debit balances in a customer's account(s) may be offset by any other outstanding balance owed by or to the customer. Please allow 4 to 6 weeks for delivery. Offer available while quantities last.

Your Privacy—The Harlequin® Reader Service is committed to protecting your privacy. Our Privacy Policy is available online at www.ReaderService.com or upon request from the Harlequin Reader Service.
We make a portion of our mailing list available to reputable third parties that offer products we believe may interest you. If you prefer that we not exchange your name with third parties, or if you wish to clarify or modify your communication preferences, please visit us at www.ReaderService.com/consumerchoice or write to us at Harlequin Reader Service Preference Service, P.O. Box 9062, Buffalo, NY 14269. Include your complete name and address.

LISDIR13R